Summer on Wheels

St. Louis de Montfort Catholic School
Fishers, IN

SCHOLASTIC INC.
New York   Toronto   London   Auckland   Sydney
Mexico City   New Delhi   Hong Kong

ISBN 0-590-48336-6
ISBN 0-439-06429-5
meets NASTA specifications

Copyright © 1995 by Gary Soto.
Cover painting © 1995 by Dan Gonzalez.
All rights reserved. Published by Scholastic Inc.
SCHOLASTIC, and associated logos and designs are trademarks
and/or registered trademarks of Scholastic Inc.
LEXILE is a trademark of MetaMetrics, Inc.

1 2 3 4 5 6 7 8 9 10   23   06 05 04 03 02 01 00

Printed in the U.S.A.

First Scholastic paperback printing, February 1999

For Yvette Garcia

CHAPTER 1

It was mid-June, and already Hector and his sidekick, Mando, were bored and without two pennies to rattle in their pockets. But they had come up with an idea: aluminum cans. They stomped soda and beer cans until the soles of their feet hurt. Now they sat on Hector's porch, sharing a cream soda. It wasn't their favorite drink, but it was something cold to throw down on a hot day.

"Man, I wish I could go to the ocean," Hector whined. He jiggled the can of soda. It was nearly empty.

"Yeah, *la playa*," Mando said dreamily.

"Yeah, me and you on one of those little surfboards," Hector said. His hand was flat and skimming over imaginary waves.

"They're called boogie boards, dude."

"Yeah, them too," Hector remarked. He looked down at the stomped cans. He figured they had about four dollars in that aluminum treasure.

Hector's mother came out on the porch, the screen door slapping against the house. She was carrying three cats: two in her arms and one squealing kitten pressed in the cup of her armpit.

"*¡Estos gatitos!*" his mother yelled. "They keep coming into the house."

"They like to watch television, Mom," Hector teased. "Especially *Sesame Street*."

"It's better for them to play in the street. *¡Ándenle!*" She lowered the cats onto the porch, and they pranced away, their shiny tails waving. She looked at the pile of crushed cans and then took the cream soda from Hector. She raised it to her mouth, swallowed the remaining drops, and crushed it with her hands. She tossed it into the pile.

"Mom," Hector said, "we're bored."

"So?" his mother said. "I'm bored of cooking and ironing. I take care of your father and you boys and these cats." She clapped at the gang of cats, who were on the hood of their family's '66 Chevy Impala. When she stomped her foot, they yawned at her. But when she picked up the broom, the cats jumped off the hood and scampered away.

"Mom, think of something for us to do," Hector said. Just as this sentence was out of his mouth, Hector realized his mistake. Hector's mom smiled at them. There was trickery in her narrowed eyes. She scanned their tiny East Los Angeles yard. The lawn was as scraggly as the back of their dog, Smiley, who was sleeping under the fig tree. Weeds poked up from the flowerbeds, where snails laced the ground with their slime trails.

"Nah, Mom, we don't want to work," Hector said as he got to his feet. "We want to do something fun."

"I want you to paint over those words," she told the boys. She referred to the fence, where *placas* made a scribbling mess. Every once in a while some kid would tag their fence with his name and the name of his gang.

Hector and Mando sighed and went to the garage, which was hot as an oven. A black halo of flies buzzed lazily in the air. They took a can of white paint and, with sloppy swishes, got rid of the graffiti. But Hector kept a small heart-shaped declaration of love: Tony and Belinda — *siempre*.

Hector had just started to like girls. He was spending more time in the bathtub, where he lay in mountains of pink bubble bath. Every night he scrubbed his throat. He had two permanent dirt rings and vowed that he would scour his neck clean, even if it became thin as a pencil. When he was twelve and saw his first pimple rise up on the tip of his nose, he didn't panic. He remembered what his cousin Yolanda had said: never, never, never squeeze a pimple or your nose will grow as fat as a water balloon.

Mando was still suspicious of girls. He figured they were tattletales and more trouble than they were worth. He didn't care if they painted over the lovers' names. He just wanted to get out of the sun and back in front of the television with one of the cats in his lap.

They were popping the lid back onto the paint can when suddenly racers on bicycles came whooshing by — hundreds it seemed, a long tail of bicyclists. They were dressed in light shorts and wearing helmets the color of tropical fruit.

"Wow," Hector said as he stepped off the curb and admired the racers.

They watched the bikes speed by. When they were out of view, Hector turned to Mando and said brightly, "Man, that's what we can do. Go on a bike trip."

"Where?" Mando asked vaguely. He was peeling flakes of paint from his knuckles.

"To Santa Monica. We can visit my aunt."

Sitting at the curb, Hector explained his plan. He had family throughout the Los Angeles area — *familia* in Pico Rivera, Maywood, Culver City,

Beverly Hills, and Santa Monica. He had an uncle living in Long Beach, just within the shadow of the ocean liner, the *Queen Mary*. But that would be out of the way, another journey for another time. Hector explained that they could bike five or ten miles each day, sleep over at a relative's house, look around like tourists, and bike some more when their welcome wore out. In five or six days they would be in Santa Monica on a beach crashing with a roll of white-tipped waves.

"Sounds like a dream life," Mando sighed. His eyes were shiny with excitement. He was looking west, where Santa Monica hugged the coast, greedily. Then his dreaminess wore off. "But I ain't got a bike, *homes*. It got stole."

"Don't worry. I got one for you."

They jumped to their feet and, carrying the paint brushes and sloshing paint can, hurried to the garage. In the far corner stood two bicycles. The boys stepped over cardboard boxes, lawn mowers, ratty lawn chairs, and old bowling trophies to get to the bicycles. The frames of the bikes were filmed over with sticky dust. Spiderwebs swung from the handlebars and between the rusty spokes.

"Hey, man, this is a girl's bike," Mando cried after a close inspection. "I can't ride it!"

"Sure you can."

"No way." Mando's face was sour with disgust. He pinched the tire, which was flat and airless.

"Who's gonna see you?"

"People."

"You don't know anyone," Hector tried to reason. "Anyway, we'll trade off. You ride the girl's bike one day and I'll ride the girl's bike the next."

Mando's face brightened. "OK, I get the dude's bike the first day."

They hauled the bicycles from the garage and hosed off the dust and spiders. They fixed the flats: the tires were now as hard as the muscles in a weight lifter's forearm. They oiled the chains and adjusted the crooked handlebars. When Hector's mother came out onto the back porch with the cats struggling in her arms, Hector looked up. He tapped Mando on the shoulder and whispered, "Now the hard part."

His mother lowered the cats onto the cement patio and scooted them with a gentle spank. She then eyed the boys, head tilted and hands on her hips. "Did you paint the fence?"

"Yes," Hector answered politely. He wasn't sure if he should ask her now or later. When one of the cats jumped onto her favorite dress drying on the clothesline and a ripping sound cut through the air, he knew it wasn't the right time. It might never be the right time.

His mother turned purple with rage. Her eyes became as fixed as the bull's-eyes of bow-and-arrow targets. She chased the cats around the yard, threatening to make slippers out of their fur.

"Let's get out of here," Hector whispered into Mando's neck. Not wanting to get involved, the boys rolled their bikes to the front yard and sat in the flickering shade of a sycamore.

"Do you think your parents will let you go?" Hector asked, sitting cross-legged.

"Yeah, if your parents do."

"I'm sure they'll let me," Hector said as he watched two cats round the corner of the house at full speed. "I think."

That night at dinner, Hector was in good form. He served the iced tea, used his napkin in little pokes around his mouth, asked politely for the tortillas bundled warmly in a dish towel, talked about his good grades in school, and smiled when his father grumbled. "The Dodgers are in last place, and getting worse!"

"But there's always next year," Hector commented.

"Yeah, it's always the same story. Next year, next year."

After dinner, Hector approached his father,

7

who sat on the front steps. His shirt was off, a roll of fat spilling over his belt. He was reading the sports section of *La Opinión*, the Spanish newspaper, by the glare of the porch light.

"Dad," Hector started to say. But he was cut off when his father ranted that the Anaheim Angels were five games under .500 and two of their starting pitchers were wearing slings. Hector heard him out. When his father calmed down, Hector started again. "Dad, me and Mando got this idea of going to Santa Monica."

His father put down his paper and asked, "¿*Qué*? Who do you know in Santa Monica?"

"Aunt Teresa. She lives pretty close."

Hector explained his plan. He started off by saying that they were bored. They hadn't had any fun since they'd visited Uncle Julio in Fresno. He said that they could bike from relative to relative and arrive at Santa Monica in four or five or, at the latest, six days. He told his father that he had called Uncle Ricardo in Maywood.

"You called your uncle Ricardo? That rascal?"

"Yeah," Hector answered brightly. Just before dinner, he had called his uncle, a sound engineer at a small, almost bankrupt record company with no hit songs or rising stars. His uncle was more than happy to let the boys stay with him for a night or two.

"Hector," his father said in a sad tone, "this is a happy moment."

"What do you mean? You don't sound happy."

"You are growing up, *mi'jo*. You are becoming a man — *un hombre!*" He sucked in his gut and the roll on his stomach collapsed an inch. "It's like when my father allowed me to herd sheep for a summer." His eyes sparkled with memory as he told Hector about the summer he and his friend Luis Moreno (better known as *Palo* for his stick-like build) herded sheep in the rugged mountains near La Junta, a town in the state of Chihuahua. By the end of the summer both boys were hardened with muscle and knowledgeable about country life.

"It sounds like you guys had fun."

"Fun's not the word, Hector, but I know what you mean."

"Then we can go?" Hector asked. He was sitting at his father's feet, hands clasped together in prayer. If he had had a tail, it would have been wagging.

"Yes, of course. It's time that you learn."

"Thanks, dad." Hector was touched by his trust. His father seldom talked to him father to son. He seldom told him about his childhood in Mexico. He seldom let him do anything adventurous. Mostly he let him pull up weeds and push the lawn mower over their lawn.

His father smiled a sneaky smile. "It also means that your mom and I can go to Las Vegas for a couple of days."

CHAPTER 2

It was not yet dawn. Hector and Mando swung their bikes from driveway to curb to a stream of water running mysteriously in the street. In the east, the rising sun was an orange splotch beneath a bank of clouds. A banged-up red Toyota pickup popped and squeaked: a husky man with hairy arms was delivering the morning edition of the *Los Angeles Times*. He tooted at the boys, and the boys waved.

They were on their way with blessings from their parents and friends and Hector's three cats: Herman, String Bean, and *Masa*. They had phoned every relative on their itinerary. Everyone was welcoming, except for *Tía* Carolina, who was in Mexico doing missionary work for her parish. They had a good send-off as they rolled from the yard. They were weighted down with heavy backpacks: clothes mostly, but also a batch of sandwiches with chips. Their pockets were lined with dollar bills. Hector also kept ten dollars in the lining of his shoe, emergency money he hoped not to spend.

They rode with Hector in the lead. His legs pumped and pumped. He couldn't stop smiling, even when a gnat was sucked into his mouth. He coughed out the gnat, wiped his mouth on his sleeve, and kept smiling. He had never felt so free. He recalled the time he took his tricycle around the block. He thought he was cool. He had just gotten out of diapers and into little boy *chones*. He remembered wearing toy sunglasses and a cowboy hat. He remembered crying when a dog barked, crying so hard that his sunglasses became splotched with tears and his thumb flew to his mouth for comfort. That was a trip, Hector thought to himself, as he smiled and ate another gnat.

"You tired?" Hector asked at a red light. A swirl of smoke from a rumbling station wagon clotted the air around them.

"No way," Mando replied, waving the smelly exhaust from his face. "*Fuchi*. That car stinks."

"They oughta crush that car. It's bad for the environment."

Hector adjusted his backpack, and when the light turned green, he shouted, "Let's go, *homes*." At this stretch, Mando took the lead. Hector was glad to ride behind. He could let

Mando watch for morning traffic and take the brunt of cursing drivers.

They rode for three miles, and when they saw the Chinese cemetery they skidded their bikes to a stop. They needed a rest, a short one, not a long one like the people buried there.

"Let's go check it out," Hector said.

They walked their bikes between the iron gates of the cemetery. The place was quiet with a wide span of grass. Not even the birds chirped. They hopped noiselessly among the headstones. In the far distance, a sprinkler revolved on the lawn. Wind sifted through the elm trees.

"It's kinda creepy," Mando said as he looked at a fresh plot.

Hector didn't say anything. He scanned the rows and rows of headstones and felt sorrow lodge in his throat. He had gone to his grandfather's funeral two years before. The crying had been endless as rain. It scared him to think that his grandfather's body was put in the ground and he would never get up again.

"You hungry?" Mando asked.

"Nah, man," Hector answered. "Just thirsty. I wish I had a snowcone."

"Me, too. Lime flavor."

They parked their bikes under a tree and plopped themselves down, more exhausted than they had realized.

"You know any scary stories?" Mando asked without looking at Hector. His attention was on two men, one Chinese and one Mexican, working a small tractor-like steam shovel: they were digging a new grave and sweating over the dead.

Hector thought for a minute. Then he remembered the story his *tía* Dolores told him.

"I know one about this lonely woman with no boyfriend," Hector started his story. The woman went to a dance, where she met a handsome man with green eyes. They danced all night. The woman was in love, and, although the man didn't say much to express his feelings, she felt that he must love her, too. Toward the end of the evening, the lights went out. The woman lost an earring during this blackout. When the lights came back on, she bent down to look for her earring. She screamed and then fainted when she saw that instead of feet and shoes, the man had chicken feet.

"I heard that one before," Mando said. "I don't believe it."

"I don't believe it either — now." Hector admitted. "But it scared me when *mi tía* told me. I was a little dude getting ready to go trick-or-treating for the first time. My aunt tole me the story and then tried to make me eat some chicken wings. I couldn't grub on *molé con pollo* for a whole year."

"My mom tole me the same chicken story when I broke my leg. She said it was gonna stay puny, and the rest of me was gonna get big." Mando laughed in his sleeve. "Then she said I was gonna lay eggs."

Hector laughed too as he imagined Mando sitting on a pile of stinky eggs. He then collected himself. He looked at Mando and then Mando's legs, which, he thought, were thin as a chicken's. Even his hair was like the comb of a chicken, straight up and wiggling when he turned his head from side to side. For a split second, he wondered if maybe, just maybe, *quién sabe*, Mando was part chicken. But Hector didn't say anything.

They tossed dirt clods into an open grave until they were chased away by the two cemetery workers. They continued their journey with Mando in the lead as he battled the traffic along Atlantic Boulevard. They passed radiator shops, tire shops, beauty parlors, a record store called *Disco Disco*, and a Kentucky Fried Chicken. Hector sniffed the good smells of fried drumsticks and looked at Mando's legs again. They *were* chicken thin and scrawny. He laughed to himself. Mando's no chicken, he thought. I've seen him fight.

Toward noon, they came across a knot of people at a corner. They slowed their bikes to a stop and studied the scene. They saw a camera, lights, and reflectors bright as chrome.

"It's Hollywood," Hector said with big eyes. "Let's check it out, homes."

They walked their bikes across the street, and they slowly nudged their way to the front of the bystanders. The director was holding a clipboard and scolding one of the actors, a girl with a set of braces that sparkled like knives. "Now you got to cry," wailed the director, who was pulling his ponytail in frustration. "Let those tears roll."

"I can't cry! I don't feel like it," the girl yelled back. Her braces flashed and her mouth twisted up in disgust.

"You're a pro, sweetie. Come on, let's cry. Boo-hoo for me."

They were shooting a Spanish-language commercial for Band-Aids. The girl was supposed to fall, scrape a knee, and reach in her pocket for a medicated Band-Aid. She was supposed to feel better after a balloon-dotted Band-Aid covered her scrape.

"I can't cry," the girl whined in Spanish.

"You're getting paid to fall and cry. You know, like money!" the director said, waving his hands.

"*I* can fall and cry, man," Hector shouted. Immediately, he threw his hand to his mouth, embarrassed. He looked around at the bystanders who were sizing him up, this loudmouth homeboy. Then he gazed up at the director.

"Who are you?" the director asked. He had stopped fiddling with his ponytail and was now clicking his Bic pen nervously. He was tall and youngish, and an earring dangled from his earlobe.

"Me?" Hector replied, pointing at himself.

The director didn't respond.

"Me?" Hector asked a second time. "I'm Hector *de East Los.*"

Again the director didn't respond. He was sizing up Hector from his feet to his wind-blown hair.

"Can you act?" the director asked.

"*Simón.* I was in a school play about cannibals. I was the dude they were going to eat." Excited, Hector turned to Mando. "Huh, homes? I can act."

"Yeah, sir, Hector's really good. I seen him cry like a diaper baby when he got beat up by Chuy Hernandez."

"See!" Hector exclaimed, beaming.

The director snapped his fingers and screamed. "You got a job! I'll pay you a hundred on the spot."

Hector would have been willing to fall over for a Big Gulp soda and two dollars. This was way better.

The director explained his role as the girl with braces pouted and started to sob real tears as she sat against the wall. The director explained that Hector would round the corner and trip on his shoelaces, hug his knee, roll up his cuffs, cry, and blow on his bruise.

"That's when you take out the Band-Aid and smile. Big smile. Like you won a trip to Disneyland."

"Yeah, or like when I won that Barney doll," Hector grinned. He recalled how he had won the stuffed doll at a church bingo game — plus a turtle keychain no bigger than his thumb. He gave that to his father for Father's Day.

"All you have to do is listen for 'Camera, speed, action.' "

"Camera, speed, action," Hector repeated. "Camera, speed, action."

"That's right. When I say 'action,' just give yourself two or three seconds, and then walk around the corner and fall."

The director turned to talk with the camera operator.

"I got it, I think," Hector whispered to himself. His heart was bloated like a frog from excitement.

A woman approached Hector. She powdered his face and combed his hair. She added a touch of color to his cheeks and for the fun of it, added a dab on Mando, who was watching with his mouth hanging open.

"We look like clowns," Mando remarked with a frown.

"We are," Hector said and hurried over to the director when he heard his name called.

The director put his arm around Hector. "Just be natural, Hector." He looked up at the sky for lighting. He took a reading with the light meter. He called for a wider lens. To Hector, the director cooed, "Go around, trip, and go through the routine. You got it?"

"I learned to trip in kindergarten. It's a piece of cake."

The director walked away from Hector, who was nervous and itchy. He wanted to scratch his nose, but he was worried about peeling off some of his makeup. Minutes passed. Bystanders looked at him. Some were eating popcorn and slurping on sodas. Then he heard, "Camera, speed, action!"

Hector breathed in a rush of dusty city air, muttered, "Here goes," and rounded the corner almost skipping. He took a few steps and threw himself into the air. He saw his life flash before his eyes. He saw his mom and dad and his three cats, plus Smiley, his lazy dog. He saw Mando and Mando's parents. He saw his dead grand-father, and each of his aunts and uncles, all of them gathered strangely around a backyard bar-becue. He felt his whole life fly like a ghost into the air, including the hundred dollars, all in ones — crisp as autumn leaves. He landed with two skips on his belly, smack against the cement. Immediately, tears leaked from his eyes, blurring his vision. He hurt, but not so much that he forgot his role. He reached into his pocket for the Band-Aids, blew on his scraped knee, and smiled through his tears for the camera.

"Cut," the director yelled with a swishing ponytail. He clapped his hands together, clapped and clapped, he was so happy. "Perfect. Perfect! Let's do it again."

CHAPTER 3

Later they rode eight more miles until dusk and arrived at Uncle Ricardo's house, a small, two-bedroom white structure. Uncle was washing his car in the front yard, a boom box near his bucket and pile of old towels. All the flowers were dead, and the screens on the windows were torn. Bees came and went as they pleased from a pyracantha bush. Uncle Ricardo, a sound engineer at a record company, was glad to see his nephew. He sprayed the boys off with the hose. A character, Uncle tried out the girl's bicycle, wobbling up and down the street while Hector and Mando finished washing the car.

Now it was nighttime. Hector sat in the bathtub, knees poking out of the water like twin peaks. A turban of bubble bath suds covered his head. He was sore all over: legs and arms and the small of his back. He hurt like a crab with all of its parts pulled off. He realized now that it was tough being an actor, tough but profitable.

He lowered his eyes to the jeans on the bathroom floor: inside the left pocket were five twenty-dollar bills with the crisp scent of success.

"Hurry up, homes," Mando shouted through the door. He rapped on the door and yelled, "Your uncle is cookin' up some grub."

"*Un momento*, bro'," Hector shouted as he rose slowly from the water. He was pink as a crab, but alive and kicking. He toweled off and slipped back into his jeans.

After he'd done the commercial, Hector had signed a few autographs and stood around waving to his admirers — four boys and girls, three old men, and a dog with one blue eye and one brown eye — before he and Mando resumed their journey. He was thanked by the director and yelled at by the girl-actor who couldn't cry. But she was crying then, and yelling that she hated boys.

Hector left the bathroom, dragging his one stiff leg.

"Smells good," Hector exclaimed, nose flaring. *"Chorizo con huevos?"*

"Con papas," said his uncle, a skinny man with a beard. He was known as *Chiva* — goat — when he was the first one in high school to grow a beard. Now he was known as Ricky, Ricardo, or Ricky Ricardo. "Mando, get the milk out," said Uncle.

While Mando poured glasses of milk and set out plates, Hector heated up flour tortillas in a black pan. When they sat down to dinner they ate in monkish silence, they were so hungry. Hector ate with his face close to the plate and only surfaced when he needed a swallow of milk.

After dinner, they sat in the living room, sleepy as three bears. Uncle put on a CD by Los Lobos and turned the volume low until the music was no louder than a whisper.

"I'm glad you guys are visiting," Uncle Ricardo said as he pulled on his beard. "I got plans for you two."

"Plans?"

"Yeah, plans," Uncle repeated.

Uncle Ricardo then explained that he needed some sound effects of two boys rapping.

"You mean like, singing, Unc?" Hector asked.

"Yeah, homey, we need two boys to kind of talk in the background." He let out a polite burp caught in the cup of his hand. He then continued: "We need some kids to whisper a little phrase, something to fill up the rap."

Hector and Mando looked at each other, big-eyed and excited. The year before when they heard Kid Frost for the first time, Hector and Mando had formed their own rap group called "He-Man," from the first letters of their names.

Their audience: the cats and dogs who congregated in the garage. Sadly, the dogs and cats ran away, and even the flies that buzzed around the ceiling vacated the place. They preferred the pile of grass clippings smoldering behind the garage.

"We're gonna make a record?" Mando asked.

"*Chale*, man, it's not exactly like that. The main rapper is Chilly Lagoon," Uncle said.

"*¿Quién es* Chilly Lagoon?" they both asked.

"He's a homeboy from Pico Rivera. He's our last chance to get down and dance! He's our brown hope to green money." Uncle Ricardo explained that the record company would fold if they didn't get a hit. Most of the singers they recorded flopped like fish on the bottom of a boat. They flopped, gasped for air, and then stunk.

"Man, here's our chance to get famous!" Hector yelled. He stood up and punched the air. He danced on his hurt leg, danced and sang the one song that they'd written, "Get Real, Banana Peel."

Mando sang along with Hector and was ready to do fancy splits when he stopped like a car skidding at a traffic light. He slapped Hector's arm and whispered into his ear. Hector shook his head.

"Mr. Salinas — " Mando started.

"Ricardo," Uncle said.

"Okay, Mr. Ricardo," Mando said business-like. "What about a contract? You know, like how much we're gonna get paid, endorsements, movie deals, health insurance, *y todo*."

Uncle looked straight-faced at the boys. He tried to keep from smiling. He ran a hand down his face and then the smile went up like a flag. "OK, let's talk."

"You first," Mando said.

"No, you first. You brought up the subject."

"*Pues*, we want ten percent, plus a nonexclusive contract and some foreign rights and stuff like that."

"You for real, *muchachos?*" Uncle laughed, his head thrown back.

"We're real," Mando said, tapping his chest with his fist and darting a look at Hector. "We're real, ain't we, homes?"

"Yeah, Unc, we're for real."

"Listen, I'll give you growing boys breakfast, lunch, and dinner for two days," Uncle said counting the days off on his fingers. "Plus those cupcakes on top of the fridge."

"That's it?" Hector sang. He flopped down on the couch, disappointed.

"That's it, nephew," his uncle answered. "We're broke. Dig this, dudes. We even have to record in the dark to save on the electric bills."

Hector and Mando huddled together and

whispered while Uncle brought out his nail clippers. He started clicking away at his fingernails and whistling "La Bamba." The boys broke from their huddle. Hector said, "OK, we got another demand."

"What? You're not asking for limousine service?" Uncle cracked.

"It's easier than that, Unc. Just throw in some *helados*, sunflower seeds, and hot *tamales*," Hector explained, "and we got a deal."

They shook on it after Uncle laughed for two minutes straight. Then the boys gobbled the cupcakes on top of the refrigerator, listened to a scratchy record of early Santana, and hopped into their bed, the pull-out sofa. All night their feet jerked as they dreamed they were dancing.

The next morning, they worked on their rap in the living room.

"OK, let me hear this song you *vatos* wrote," Uncle asked. Unshaven and in his bathrobe, he sat cross-legged with a cup of coffee. The sports section was in his lap, folded on another defeat of the Los Angeles Dodgers. They were six games behind .500, and getting worse.

Hector remembered the words, but was too embarrassed to sing them. He slapped Mando on the arm and growled, "You sing, dude."

"Nah, man," Mando said. "You sing 'em. You

wrote most of them 'cause you spell better than me."

Hector gulped and looked at his uncle. He stood up, breathed in and out, and with a "here-goes" look on his face, sang, "Get real, you banana peel/jump in a car and let's make it far/ *chale ese*/mama calls, bad boys *chamacos*/get inside 'cause you got some tacos/you can't go 'cause your grades be too low/*eesseeeeeeeee*/Get real, banana peel/school's not the place, I says/for the cool to be a fool."

Breathing hard and smiling, Hector stopped and took a stage bow. He smiled at his uncle, who was sitting in his recliner, eyes closed.

"What do you think?" Hector asked.

His uncle didn't say anything. He was sleeping, it appeared, a baby snore starting to rattle from his nose. After a moment, his eyes fluttered open, thin as a shark's, and he remarked, "Nice rap, homeboy, whatever it means."

"It means, 'be cool.' It's a message song."

"I like that message. But I got news for you dudes. No singing, just talking."

"We're not gonna sing?"

Uncle sipped his coffee and said, "Nope. Chilly Lagoon is the dude who's gonna' do the singing. I got other plans for you two canaries."

Uncle dressed and splashed himself with cologne. They left the house with their cheeks stuffed with cupcakes. On the way to the studio, in a rattling Dodge Dart with buckled fenders, Uncle explained that Chilly Lagoon's rap was about baseball and all he wanted the boys to chant was "pop-up in the infield/drop pop-up in the bleachers."

"That's all?" Hector asked, his face pinched up in a questioning look.

"That's it. *Nada más.*"

"Can we renegotiate our contract?" Mando asked.

"You guys are taking me to the cleaners. Wiping me out and it's only the middle of the month," Uncle said as he turned onto Atlantic Boulevard. His knuckles were bone-white on the steering wheel.

"Nah, don't worry. I think we overcharged you. You can drop the hot tamales."

The recording studio was a pink building that was once a French dry cleaners. The burnt-out neon sign above the front door read, "A Clean Fold, the French Way." They got out of the car. Hector looked at Mando and Mando looked at a guy pushing a cart up the street. The man was singing "La Bamba."

"Poor, dude," Mando muttered. *"Quién sabe,* homes. He could be an old rock star."

They shrugged their shoulders and entered

the studio. Uncle yelled, "Hello! *¡Hola!*" No one answered, but *"hola"* echoed off the wall. Uncle checked the answering machine. He played it back and the voice on the end snapped, "This is Mr. Taylor from the county! We haven't received summer payment for your business license. We're asking — "

"What a joker," Uncle giggled. "A business associate."

He erased the message before it was finished. He then prodded the boys and showed them the office, cluttered with piles of CDs and records and an unwatered plant shrugging off its last leaves. He showed the boys the bathroom. When Hector tried the light switch, it didn't work.

"Yeah, we gotta get lightbulbs when a check comes in," Uncle said. He led them next to the recording studio, which was dark and stank of cigarette smoke. There were mattresses tacked to the four walls.

"Who sleeps on the wall, Unc?" Hector joked.

"Couple of Chicano vampires," Uncle laughed. He told them that the mattresses were used for soundproofing. He said that one mattress once belonged to Elvis Presley.

"You're foolin' with us, Unc," Hector said, clicking his tongue.

"*De veras*, homey. And that fat one belonged to Fred Flintstone."

Uncle showed off the machine where the sounds were mixed. To Hector, it seemed like the knobs were for a low-riding spaceship. There were a hundred knobs and he wondered if his uncle really knew how to use them. He didn't ask. He was beginning to feel sad for his uncle, a good dude but poor as a sparrow.

Uncle rehearsed their lines for ten minutes and then snapped earphones on their heads. He placed a microphone on a table, pushed it in front of the boys, and told them not to move. Then he hurried away and took his place at the soundboard. He flipped a switch and called, "When I give you a hand signal, you dudes start whispering, 'Pop-up in the infield, pop-up in the bleachers.' Keep rapping until I say to stop. *¿Entienden?*"

The boys nodded their heads. Hector looked at the microphone, his palms sweaty. He was scared. He remembered the talent show in fourth grade when he sang "Oh, Donna" to the entire school. He sang the song even though his friends had lifted up their eyelids and folded them inside out, which made him feel sick.

"Again, I just want you *vatos* to talk, not sing," Uncle said. "Maybe you can kinda whisper, like you're saying confession."

The boys nodded their heads and waited nervously for the hand signal.

"Let's do it right," Hector whispered. "Looks like skid row in this place."

"*Órale.* I know what you mean," Mando agreed. He was looking up at a clock that had stopped at 3:13.

When the signal came, the boys whispered in unison, whispered because they knew their reward was the sweetness of candy and *helados*. For Uncle, it was the sweetness of a hit song. Hector didn't want his uncle to have to pull one of the mattresses off the wall and sleep in the street.

CHAPTER 4

That night, Uncle Ricardo maneuvered his Dodge Dart over a pothole larger than a food bowl for a St. Bernard. The back tire clipped the edge, and the car squeaked and rocked.

"This is fun," Hector said, his head wagging like a balloon on his shoulders.

"Yeah, it's a lot of fun," Uncle agreed, his eyes watching for the next pothole, this one smaller. "I got recaps on this baby."

They were in the parking lot of Dodger Stadium. The Dodgers were playing the San Francisco Giants, and unless lightning struck the Giant's dugout, where Barry Bonds sat clipping his fingernails, the Dodgers didn't have a chance. They parked the car, grabbed a blanket for the cold, and stashed some sodas in their jacket pockets. Hector shouldered a plastic trash bag stuffed with popcorn.

"This is fun," Mando said. "I only been to two

Dodger games. They play really good even when they lose."

Uncle fingered the tickets, free ones from a client in exchange for some CDs and records. Uncle felt he got the better deal, even though the seats were way up near the lights. He figured that if they stood up, they could probably touch the Goodyear Blimp if it should pass.

With Uncle in the lead, the three of them hurried toward the gate. The game was ready to start as a country-western singer was yodeling "The Star-Spangled Banner."

"*¡Ándale!*" Uncle called. "Wait 'til we get seated before you start on the popcorn."

Hector and Mando's cheeks were fat as two squirrels gobbling on acorns. When Hector shouted, "We're coming, Unc," a wet popcorn flew from his mouth.

"*Asco,*" Mando laughed, spitting out his own share of popcorn.

Chuckling, they trotted toward the gate, where a vendor wrapped in an apron was yelling, "Souvenirs! Programs!" When they approached the gate, a cameraman shouldered his video camera and suddenly its light was on them. Hector didn't know what to think as he pushed his body through the turnstile and a man in a blue blazer pointed and said, "You! Young man!"

Hector thought of running, a reflex from living in the *barrio*. It was the same reflex whenever he saw a brown, official-looking car and neighbors shouted, *"¡La Migra!"* But he just pointed a thumb at himself and said, "Me?"

"Yes, you."

The cameraman hovered over Hector. Another man licked a pencil and flipped open a notepad.

"Hey, what's going on?" Uncle snarled. "We just got popcorn in the trash bag! We're clean, homes." He patted his jacket and admitted, "These are just a couple of cold sodas."

"Yeah, sir," Mando interrupted. "Just a twenty-five-cent Safeway root beer from the machine in the front."

Hector blinked from the glare of the camera. When the man with the notepad asked Hector's name, Hector tottered back on the heels of his tennis shoes. Now he was sure that he was in trouble. He was wondering how they knew that he had put a *placa* — graffiti — on his own wall. Maybe Mom turned me in, Hector thought.

"What's going on?" Uncle asked a second time, his voice ragged with anger. "You got nothin' on us."

"Your boy here," the man said, placing a hand on Hector's shoulder. "He's the millionth attendee."

"Huh?" Hector asked. "I'm not even in seventh grade. How can I be . . . a what-you-call-it . . . millionth attendee?"

Uncle caught on immediately. His eyes grew as big as the potholes in the parking lot. He knew that they were royalty. "Nephew, you hit the jackpot. Put down the popcorn!" He gave Hector an *abrazo*, a great big hug. He hugged Mando, too, who let out a spray of half-chewed popcorn. He shook the man's hand nearly a million times. He pulled the sodas from his jacket and pushed them into the hands of a security officer. "Here, these sodas are on us!"

Hector was the millionth fan, and he and his party — Uncle and Mando — were being treated to a luxury box.

"You mean, like, we won something?" Hector smiled.

"The best seats in the house." The man smiled back.

While they were ushered away, Hector was interviewed by a newspaper reporter. He was asked his age, his school, his parents' names, his all-time favorite player (it was really Willie Mays of the Giants but he said Fernando Valenzuela), his favorite food (chicken *molé*), favorite movie (*Raiders of the Lost Ark*), and his best friend (Mando spoke up and said "me"), his favorite teacher, and the name of his Little League team.

They climbed two series of steps. Hector was grinning and waving to people as he marched up and up. He could hear the crowd booing. He figured that Barry Bonds, the slugger of sluggers, was coming up with a man or two on base.

"Here's your box," the man said, opening the door for them. The man, middle-aged with wings of gray at his temples, was breathing hard from the climb. He unbuttoned his blue blazer and wiped his forehead with the back of his hand.

The three of them stepped into the luxury box along with a reporter, a young man with a dangling earring shaped like a baseball bat. On a table, there was an array of food — cold cuts and fruits, sesame bread, carrot cake, and a carousel of fat Polish weenies. In the corner, between two healthy palm trees straight as soldiers, sat a tub of icy cold sodas. Two small television sets broadcast the game.

"I can't believe this," Hector said as he stabbed a strawberry with a toothpick. He pushed it into the cavern of his mouth and next tried a slice of cantaloupe, a heavier piece of fruit, which nearly snapped the toothpick.

"You are a lucky person," the man chuckled. "I'll be back later. Enjoy the game." He closed the door behind him as he left.

"This is sweet," Uncle whistled as he popped

open a soda and handed it to Hector. He tossed one to Mando and another to the reporter.

Hector hurried to the window and scanned the playing field. Still in the first inning, the Dodgers were on the field, which was deep green under the stadium lights. The flags waved in a westerly breeze. A faraway plane motored the twilight skies, and seagulls screeched as they circled against the dry hills. Hector pinched himself. But he knew he was alive when he took a swig from his cherry soda and his nostrils burned from bubbles of carbonation. He backhanded his mouth and said, "Yeah, Unc, this is sweet."

With the others, Hector fixed himself a sandwich — a pile of turkey, pastrami, and ham on a wheat bun. He dotted his concoction with pickles and a single ring of onion. He then filled another plate with fruit and picked up handfuls of barbecue-flavored potato chips. He took his grub to the window.

"This is good stuff," Mando said just before he threw his face into a sandwich.

"You got it right, homes," Hector agreed.

It was now the bottom of the second inning, and the Dodgers were up. A batter popped up quietly and suddenly it was the top of the third before Hector even took two healthy bites from his heavyweight sandwich. Just as he was about to raise his soda to his lips, Barry Bonds hit a foul ball that landed in the row of seats in front of them.

"I bet you can't do that again!" Mando yelled through his mouth filled with food.

The next pitch — a foul — rose at the crack of the bat. With his mouth open, Hector watched the ball sail toward them like a fist and ducked when it smashed against the plexiglass window of their luxury box. For a second, the television reception was scrambled.

"*Chihuahua!*" Uncle cried. "Have mercy."

"Hey, man, I was only talkin' trash," Mando apologized, cowering behind the table.

After eating, they settled down to watch the game, which went cleanly. There were no dramatic plays. No one slid, no one dived for the ball, no one went down on one knee to gobble up a hit. The Giants took a 3–0 lead off a homer from Will Clark, and it stayed that way until the Dodgers clipped the lead by one run.

In the meantime, between innings, the reporter interviewed Hector about school, his friends, his family, his favorite sports — getting facts that would fill a five-inch column about that year's millionth fan. He took a photograph of Uncle hugging Hector and Mando.

"Does your mother know you're here?" the

reporter asked, his pencil wagging in his hand. He uncrossed his legs and reached for his soda.

"Nah, she's in East Los," Hector said. "Me and Mando are taking a bike trip. It's kinda like our vacation."

"Why don't you call her from here?" the reporter suggested. He pointed to the red telephone on a far table. "The game is being televised."

Hector looked at his unc, who said, "*Qué buena idea.* Call up my sis, your momma, and that daddy of yours."

Hector scrambled for the telephone and dialed his home number. He was laughing to himself. His mother would never guess where he was. On the third ring, his mom answered with a sleepy, "*¿Bueno?*"

"It's me, Mom," Hector shouted excitedly.

"*¿Quién?*"

"Me. Hector, you know, your son."

For a moment there was silence. Hector could hear cats running around the living room, hissing. Then she scolded, "Hector! Did you know that you forgot to take a pen out of your pocket and now your *chones* are all blue."

"Speaking of blue, Mom," he said, ignoring her complaint. "Guess where we are?"

"Don't tell me you're in juvie?"

"Nah, Mom, we're at Dodger Stadium. We got a free luxury box with all the grub we can stuff in our faces."

"*¡De veras!*" Mando shouted in the background. He handed Hector a second sandwich that was fat as a baseball mitt.

"Liar!" Hector's mom scolded. "Where are you? Are you in trouble?"

Uncle took the telephone from Hector and said, "Hey, *hermana*, it's your bad brother."

"Ricardo?"

"Yeah, the one and only. We hit it rich today, sis. We got our box and grub for days."

He explained their fortune and then said, "Turn on the TV, *hermana*, and check out the scene. Where's your old man, your little fat hubby?"

"He's watering the front lawn."

"Tell him to get inside and see for himself."

Hector got back on the telephone and heard his Mom yell, "*Viejo*, it's Hector and my brother Ricky. I think they're up to no good."

When Hector's father came on, breathing hard from the climb up the steps, Hector explained their fortune. He asked him to take the telephone to the living room and turn on the television.

"That's real good, *mi'jo*," his father cooed.

"I wish you were here, *Papi*," Hector said. His father seldom went to baseball games. Instead, he followed them on the Spanish-language radio.

"Me, too. I guess it's too late to get over there."

"Yeah, it's already the sixth inning."

Hector's mother yelled that the television was on, but that she couldn't see them.

"Where are you?" she asked.

"Mom, there are fifty thousand people. You can't see us," Hector explained.

But right then, the TV sports announcer said, "We have our millionth fan for the season, folks. It's Hector Molina from East Los Angeles. This young lad and his friends get the private use of a luxury box."

The camera turned on their luxury box, where Hector, Mando, and Uncle were waving to the thousands of spectators. For a second, Hector felt like a baseball player — famous! He still had the telephone cradled to his ear. He heard his mom say proudly, "*Mi'jo*, it *is* you! And that sandwich looks really good."

CHAPTER 5

They spent two days at Uncle's house playing handball against his garage, and then they were on the road again. The next stop: Hector's *Tía* Helena and *Tío* Eloy in Culver City, a fifteen-mile ride. They thanked Uncle a thousand times, and Uncle warned, "OK, *chamacos*, watch out for the traffic." He waved from the porch. "I'll keep you *vatos* posted about Chilly Lagoon. We're counting on him."

They rode quickly, their legs pumping the pedals, and traded bikes when they thought they were halfway there. They stopped at a small park to rest. There, they joined a crowd watching a Mexican magician. He pulled scarves from his ears and his fist. With a tap of a wand, he changed clear water into blue water and blue water into red water. He tore newspapers into shreds no bigger than confetti and threw them into the air — abracadabra! — the newspaper once again became a front page full of bad news about wars and unemployment.

"He's good," Mando said, lapping on a diminishing Tootsie Roll Pop. He clapped and whistled so loud that his Tootsie Roll shot from his mouth.

"*Asco,*" Hector scolded.

"Sorry, homes," Mando said, chuckling. He thought of picking up the candy but left it there.

Next, the magician pulled a snake from a sack and let it crawl up his arm into his long hair. The snake disappeared and then appeared slithering from his pants cuff.

"He's *bad,*" Hector said to Mando. "I wish I could do that."

When the magician asked for something precious, Hector waved his hand and yelled, "*Señor,* how about this?" He searched his backpack and brought out a picture that Tommy Lasorda had autographed for him.

"*Mira,*" the performer announced to the crowd as he pranced around like a chicken. "*Un autógrafo de* Tommy Lasorda, head of the Dodgers."

The magician smiled at Hector, a front tooth winking gold. He swiftly tore the picture of Tommy Lasorda in two, then into quarters, and then little pieces. He rubbed the pieces together in his hands, turned away from the crowd, and huddled into himself like Dracula. Then, leaping forward, he waved an unblemished picture of a smiling Tommy Lasorda.

Hector watched, dumbfounded, his jaw slack, and reached for the photograph. He took it from the magician. Except for a small tear in the corner, the photograph was as it had been.

The boys left the park and continued their journey, dodging cars and kicking away barking dogs that tried to nip their pants legs. They ate sandwiches as they rode and swigged on sodas. They spit sunflower seeds into the wind of traffic and biked through sprinklers to cool off. They made it to Hector's *tía* and *tío's* house in Culver City just before one o'clock. They were exhausted. Their legs were as wobbly as restaurant chairs.

"*Tía! Tío!* We're here," Hector yelled as he climbed off his bike, *nalgas* hurting. He let the backpack slide from his shoulders onto the lawn. He fanned himself with his baseball cap.

"Nice place," Mando chimed, letting his bike fall onto the lawn. The house was two-storied with a fountain of Poseidon, the Greek god of the sea, gurgling water from his mouth. "What do your aunt and uncle do?"

"They got good jobs," Hector said. "My uncle

is an engineer or something. I don't know what my aunt does."

They walked up to the front door. "I also got a cousin, but I haven't seen him since he and I were babies."

Hector knocked on the door and poked a finger at the doorbell five times. His cousin Bentley answered the door, holding a book in his hands. He was smaller than either Hector or Mando. He wore glasses and a necktie as thin as a noodle.

"*¿Qué pasa?*" Hector greeted. "Hey, homes! I haven't seen your mug since you and me were truckin' around the yard in our underwear. *¿Recuerdas?*"

"I'm afraid I don't recall," Bentley said, pushing open the screen door and extending a hand. "However, we've been expecting you." Hector shook his hand *raza*-style, a twist of finger moves that left Bentley confused.

"And this dude is my number one *carnal*, Mando," Hector said with a big smile. But his smile collapsed into a thin line when he saw that Mando had a sunflower seed shell pasted to his cheek. "Hey, dude, wipe your face."

Mando's hands searched his forehead and then his cheek. He picked off the shell and flicked it away.

"That's better," Hector said. "Like I say, this is Mando. I've known himself since we were in kindergarten."

"Hey, dude," Mando said, smiling. *"Mucho gusto."*

"It is a pleasure to meet you . . . Mando," Bentley said politely. "Please come in. We have refreshments and a light buffet."

When Bentley turned away, Mando looked at Hector and mouthed in a whisper, "Refreshments and a light buffet?"

Hector elbowed Mando to be quiet. But he could see that Bentley had changed from the time when everyone called him "Little Benny." The baby that he remembered was a neighborhood kid with scabs on his chubby knees. Now he seemed like a nerd of some kind. Hector glanced down at the book Bentley was holding in the crook of his arm. It was Shakespeare's *Romeo and Juliet.*

The cool air in the house sent a chill through Hector. They had been riding for two hours and coming from the L.A. heat into the air-conditioned house forced Hector to sneeze.

"Gesundheit," Bentley said.

"Salud," Mando said.

"Where's *mi tía*?" Hector asked, craning his neck and looking around.

"She's at the hospital."

46

"She sick?"

Bentley adjusted his eyeglasses on his nose. "No, Hector, she is not ill. My mom is a physician, as you may remember."

Bentley gestured with an open hand and said, "Perhaps you'd care to freshen up?"

"Yeah, we think we better wash the smog off our faces, huh, dude?" Hector said, elbowing Mando. Mando nodded his head and smiled.

Hector and Mando disappeared into the bathroom.

"What's the matter with your *primo*?" Mando asked, running the faucet. "He's a strange *vato*."

"I don't know, homes. I think he's like a genius or something. But he's cool."

"Yeah, he's polite and all, but he don't seem like us." Mando picked up the bathroom reading, a copy of *Scientific American*. "They read this kinda stuff?"

"Well, homes, it takes all kinds. We're in his house, so we better respect it." Hector dried his face on a towel and nearly leaped out of his tennis shoes when he saw that he had left an imprint of his dirty face. He held up the towel to Mando, who muttered, "*¡Qué feo!*"

They washed up and then followed their noses to the dining room, where Bentley was popping the cork off a dark green bottle. Mando looked at the spread of food — goose liver pâté, brie,

Camembert, Bremner wafers, carved radishes, and midget pickles. For dessert, there was a strawberry cheese torte.

"Looks good, Bentley," Hector said, rubbing his palms together like a fly. "Is that *champagne*?"

"No, it's sparkling cider," Bentley corrected. He poured three glasses and handed Hector and Mando each a glass.

Hector put his ear to the glass. "I like the way it bubbles."

"Yeah, man, but don't drink through your ear, homes," Mando warned with a laugh. He hooked his thumb toward his lips and said, "It's supposed to go in your mouth."

"Shut up!" Hector scolded lightly. "I just like the sound. I know how to drink it."

Bentley chimed, "Cheers," and raised his long-stemmed champagne glass. The boys clinked and Hector and Mando downed it all in one long swallow, while Bentley took a proper sip. He told the boys to help themselves. Hector and Mando got to work, piling their plates with food. They sat down and ate and talked with their mouths full.

"So what are you doin' this summer?" Hector asked Bentley.

"Well, I'm mostly reading Shakespeare and taking a course in organic chemistry in a summer program at the college," Bentley replied. He dabbed the corner of his mouth with a napkin and burped. "I also have a tutor in Latin that I meet once a week."

Mando looked at Hector and Hector looked at Mando. They were beginning to wonder about Bentley.

"So you like to study, huh?" Hector asked.

"I enjoy learning," Bentley agreed.

"But don't you ever play?" Mando asked. "Like baseball or soccer or even four square?"

"No," Bentley said, almost apologizing. "But I would like to live a more physical life. For instance, I wouldn't mind learning to . . ." his voice trailed off. He had an embarrassed look on his face as he busied himself nibbling a cracker.

"*¿Qué, primo?* You can level with us homeboys."

"Well, I wouldn't mind learning to ride a bicycle."

"Hey, man, we can help you out," Hector said, standing up. He suddenly felt sorry for his cousin, a genius who didn't know how to play. He swiped a handful of crackers and three midget pickles, and yelled, "Let's go, homes."

The three of them got up and went outside.

As he approached the bicycles on the front lawn, Hector said, "But first, Bentley, you got to get rid of that tie. It might get caught in the spokes."

Bentley undid his tie and stuffed it in his pants pocket.

"Next, you got to take the handlebars like the horns of a bull, pedal, and use your weight to stay up."

Bentley straddled the girl's bike. "You think I can do it?"

"*Claro*," Hector scolded. "You're a genius."

"*Simón*," Mando encouraged. "Like your *primo* says, just keep things in check. Balance is the name of the game."

"And don't worry," Hector added. "We'll run next to you and if you look like you're gonna fall, we'll set you straight. *¿Entiendes*, Mendez?"

Bentley nodded his head. He breathed in and out and sighed, "Here goes." He pushed down one pedal and started off with a wobble. The bike maneuvered unsteadily across the lawn onto the sidewalk, the spokes catching the sunlight. Hector and Mando followed, yelling that it was a piece of cake.

"Go, brown boy, go," Hector screamed. "You got it?"

"Wow, I'm riding!" Bentley screamed joyfully.

He rode up the block, face straining with each kick of the pedal. But as he rounded the corner, the bike hit the curb and Bentley went over the handlebars, his eyes closed but one hand saluting Hector and Mando. "I'm flying," he yelled with an even deeper joy just before he landed with a belly flop on the trimmed lawn of a neighbor's yard.

CHAPTER 6

Bentley sat at the kitchen table running an ice cube back and forth across the knot on his forehead. The knot was like a speed bump. The ice cube glided across smooth skin before it jumped up and over the knot. Bentley whimpered like the puppy he was. He had flown over the handlebars and not only hurt his head, but also scraped his elbows and chin. And the air left his lungs when he belly flopped. It took a full minute before he could get enough air back into his system to complain, "Golly, that smarted."

Hector peeked at Bentley's swollen lump. He recalled when he was in a dirt-clod war with some other kids from his neighborhood. He had gotten cornered and when one of the enemies aimed a dirt clod, Hector bowed his head, so that the top of his skull became a shield. Like a good soldier, he took the blow without flinching. The thud echoed in his ears and vibrated all the way down to his dirty toes. No matter how much he cried, the tears could not cool his anger and shame.

"You'll be OK," Hector cooed. "We're always getting hurt, huh, Mando?"

"All the time, homes. Shoot, just before me and Hector left on our trip, man, I was putting on my dad's cologne and got some in this eye." He pulled open his right eye with his fingers and rotated the eyeball for Hector and Bentley.

"*Asco*," Hector laughed. "You got the evil eye."

Hector tossed an ice cube into his mouth and was sucking on it when the front door opened and *Tía* Helena — Bentley's mother — greeted them. "I'm home. Bentley? Hector?"

Hector choked on the ice cube, choked and coughed. Mando spanked his back to dislodge the cube from his throat. Hector spat it out just as his aunt came into the kitchen, a stethoscope around her neck. The ice cube hit her in the arm, ricocheting off the wall.

"I'm sorry, *Tía* Helena," Hector cried, horrified. He hadn't seen his aunt in three years and the first thing he did was spit an ice cube at her.

"Hello, Hector," she coolly greeted him as she tossed the ice cube into the sink. She looked at Bentley and asked, "Bentley, is something wrong?"

"Well, Mom, I took a spill," Bentley answered. "Hector and Mando — "

"That's me," Mando said, pulling up the corners of his mouth into a smile.

"Hector and Mando," Bentley continued, "taught me how to ride a bike — sort of."

"Ride a bike! You were on a bike?" Tía said with surprise. "And now you're hurt, I take it?"

"Just a little bit," Bentley said, his puppy eyes floating up to his mother's worried look. "But it was fun, Mommie."

She took her son's head into her hands and examined the knot, which was knuckle-hard. "And what is this on your chin?"

"It's the same as on my elbows." He raised his elbows and showed her the twin scrapes.

Tía Helena wagged her head and clicked her tongue. She looked at her nephew, eyes narrowed into flints of anger. She looked ready to scold, but instead said calmly, "Hello, Hector. I haven't seen you in years." She gave her nephew a hug, a pat on his head, and pulled on his cheek tenderly.

"And who is this — Mando?" his *tía* asked.

"That's me," Mando replied. "I'm Hector's number one *carnal*."

She shook his hand and said, "Welcome, Mando. We're very glad to meet you and to have you in our home."

"Thank you, *señora*," he said, shaking her hand, *raza*-style.

That night the family sat down to dinner after Bentley's father came home. Flowers decorated the table and two tall candles wavered in the breeze of the air conditioning. They started dinner with a salad course, which worried Hector because he wasn't sure which fork to use — the small one or the slightly bigger one. He decided to alternate between the two, figuring that he would be wrong only half the time.

"We're glad you and Mando are visiting us," *Tío* Eloy said. He was distinguished-looking. He had been wearing a suit and tie when he got home, and now he was wearing a sweater and tie, just like Bentley, who also wore Band-Aids on his forehead and chin. He looked pale, like a poster boy for sick children.

"We're glad to be here. Huh, Mando?" Hector said, his fork poked with carrots.

"Right on," Mando responded without looking up, his lips curved around a bun.

"And I understand that you taught Bentley how to ride a bicycle," his *tío* beamed.

"Yeah, it was easy," Hector said. "But Bentley has to learn how to use more balance."

"You're quite right — balance," *Tío* Eloy remarked seriously. "That's what our son needs in his life, a balance between the physical and the intellectual worlds." He wiped his mouth and pushed back his chair. "Bentley is a very smart boy, as you may have discovered, but he hasn't had — how can I say this without being impertinent — a typical childhood. He needs to experience the everyday."

Hector looked at Mando, who was holding a fork in each hand, a switch-hitter at the dinner plate. Hector wished Mando would slow down on the chow a bit.

"I was thinking that perhaps you might teach Bentley how to do ordinary things," *Tía* Helena interrupted.

"Yes, 'ordinary things,' " *Tío* said, his hands folded softly over his cloth napkin.

"You mean, stuff like me and Mando do?" Hector asked,

"Yes, that's it," his *tío* said. "Just being boys."

"Like playing and goofing around."

"Exactly!" both parents cried.

Hector put down his fork and looked at Bentley, who seemed eager. Hector liked his cousin and liked the idea of tripping around in Culver City for a day or two more. He looked at his smiling aunt and uncle. He looked at Mando, who was eager only for more of the roast beef he'd herded into a raggedly sliced bun.

"Let's go for it then, Bentley," Hector cried. "Let's get going now!"

Hector stood up and undid Bentley's tie, then ripped off his Band-Aids and said "ouch" for his cousin.

After dinner, Hector taught Bentley how to wrestle on the front lawn. First he got Mando into a chicken arm-bar and then a sleeper. Then he body-slammed Mando on the lawn, who rose up on his elbows with grass in his mouth. He got him into a half nelson and flopped him over like a fish. Drool leaked from Mando's mouth.

"See," Hector said, breathing hard. "It's easy. Just use your weight. And if you been eating something smelly like *chicharrones*, use that to your advantage. Breathe on 'em. Stink up the air, homes. They usually give up."

They spent an hour wrestling, and after Bentley was pinned twenty times by both Hector and Mando, they gave him a breather. They taught him how to shake hands, *raza*-style, and the hand signals for "watch out." They taught him to walk with a swagger in his hips and to stand, one leg kicked out and his hands in his pockets, looking like a bad dude.

"And Bentley," Hector said, circling him. "I don't want to offend you, homey, but you got to get a new name." Hector looked at Mando, who nodded his head and said, "Let's call him 'Little Benny,' like he was before."

"That's sweet," Hector said.

"Me? 'Little Benny'?" Bentley muttered, pointing at himself.

"Yeah, Little Benny *de* Culver City."

The next morning, after Little Benny's parents went to work (*Tía* was called to an emergency at the hospital), Hector took his pupil outside. The morning sun was raking the dew off the front lawn. Three sparrows were quarreling in the silk tree that stood at the side of the house. A neighbor was washing his car, occasionally glancing at the three boys.

"OK, homes, let's learn the ABC's of walking on a fence," Hector said. "And don't wear your *pantalones* all the way to your chest, homey." Hector wiggled Bentley's pants down so that they hung on his hips. "*¡Ándale!* Climb up!"

"But Mother doesn't allow me to climb on the fence," Little Benny said.

"Mommie ain't home."

"But I'm scared of heights."

"No you ain't. Just do it!"

So Little Benny learned to walk a fence, eyes closed, and learned how to jump from the roof and roll without getting hurt. He learned to ride a bike, climb a tree, kick a soccer ball, chew gum and sunflower seeds at the same time and, with a baseball cap flipped backwards, yell, "*¡Órale!* Get down, *carnal*."

They returned to the house, hot from goofing around. Hector then showed Little Benny how to make a *quesadilla* using pieces of bologna, and to slam jam on crackers, the dessert of poor people. Afterwards, he fit some socks on Little Benny's fists and said, "Let's box!"

"You mean, like, hit each other?"

"*Claro que sí*, Little Einstein. A time may come when you have to defend yourself."

They boxed in the living room — jab, jab, and poke to the belly. Little Benny's nose bled in no time, but so did Hector's when Little Benny connected with a wild roundhouse punch.

"Good shot," Hector cried, eyes watering.

They bled on each other's shirts and then fixed themselves another round of *quesadillas*, this time with a slash of peanut butter.

"Oh, no," Little Benny said, palming the front of his brain-jammed forehead. "I forgot to do my Latin!"

"You forgot you're Latino," Hector laughed.

Little Benny looked at his cousin, feelings hurt. He got up and left the kitchen, shoulders hunched.

"Just jokin', dude," Hector called through the peanut butter stuck in his mouth. When Little Benny returned with his Latin book, Hector asked, "How come you're so smart?"

"It's a matter of study," Little Benny answered as he plopped open his book. *"Fortiter nobis pugnandum est."*

"¿Qué?" Mando said. "Speak English, *carnal."*

"Yeah, what does that mean?" Hector asked. "Sounds like you were talking backwards."

"It means, 'We must fight bravely.' "

"Say it again," Hector demanded, eyes dancing with light. He nodded his head and cooed, "Man, that's sweet. Write that down on a piece of paper. I'll use it back in the *barrio."*

Little Benny wrote it down and then did his homework while Hector and Mando watched television, a rerun of *Gilligan's Island* that to them was funnier the second time around. Then they left for the playground, where Hector taught Little Benny first how to bunt and then how to slam fly balls. He taught him how to slide without burning his *nalgas* and then, when three other boys came by, Hector whispered, *"Fortiter nobis pugnandum est."* He challenged the boys to play football using a fluorescent-green tennis ball. The boys accepted with sneers on their faces. In the afternoon sun, they plowed into each other, ruined the knees of their pants, and sweated buckets.

"I got it," Little Benny cried on one play, his mouth open. But the ball bounced off his fingertips and he was scissored by a leg.

"Hey, dude," Hector yelled, "you can't do that to *mi primo*."

The boy who had scissored said, "Shut up, man."

"*Fortiter nobis pugnandum est,*" Hector yelled, fists closed as he approached the boy. Hector spit a mouthful of sunflower seeds at the boy, momentarily confusing him, and then pushed him to the ground. A fight broke out, and arms and legs began to fan the afternoon air.

"Your momma," Hector yelled and jabbed to his opponent's chest.

"But your momma too," the boy yelled back as he clipped Hector on the chin.

Hector, Mando, and Little Benny lost by three touchdowns and some blood as well. They returned home, smothering their bloody noses with their shirts.

"How did I do?" Little Benny asked as he washed his face in the bathroom sink. His cheek was red from a punch and his neck was scratched.

"Great," Hector said, dabbing his nostrils with a Kleenex.

"Yeah," Mando agreed, then added, as he raised Little Benny's head. "*Míra*, he's got two dirt rings on his throat."

"All right," Hector yelled. "It's like a tattoo."

Little Benny admired his throat and its two

rings of dirt. He was happy. He said to the mirror, *"Tela comparavit ad pugnandum."* Holding up his fists, he translated the sentence for Hector and Mando. "It means something like I've got weapons for fighting."

"De veras," Hector said, slapping his cousin on the back.

They cleaned up and then raided the refrigerator. This time, instead of *quesadillas*, they poked black olives on their wagging fingers and ate them one by one like cannonballs.

CHAPTER 7

That night at dinner Hector taught Little Benny how to poke holes in tortillas and use them for masks, their tongues flipping about like wild snakes. They played with their food until Little Benny's parents — *Tía* Helena and *Tío* Eloy — told them to knock it off or they would have to take their plates and eat in the bathroom.

"Sorry," Hector apologized. He gave a hand signal to his cousin that meant, *"la policía,"* and the boys giggled.

Later that evening Hector got a call from his Uncle Isaac in Beverly Hills. Uncle Isaac, who worked as a chauffeur for a lawyer, had promised Hector and Mando that they could stay in his cabin, which was hidden away behind a mansion. But now he was asking them to show up one day later than planned. This suited Hector and Mando because Little Benny had invited them to spend a day at the college where he was taking chemistry. Hector figured they could kick around while Little Benny played Dr. Chicano Frankenstein with test tubes and bubbling concoctions.

The next morning, they took off for Loyola Marymount University, a six-mile ride. Little Benny rode on the handlebars, his fists knuckle-white from fear because within a block from home, Hector hit a curb and Little Benny popped off like a rocket. He flew into the air, scattering his homework that was the chicken scratching of high math.

But the rest of the six-mile ride was as smooth as a new road. They stopped once for a soda when, sitting at a curb, Mando asked, "So what do you do in college?"

"Well, Mando, it's not *really* college. It's a college preparatory course for the academically talented."

"You like that kinda stuff?" Hector asked. He backhanded sweat from his eyes and said, "I'm pretty talented at math myself and I even got a B in algebra."

"You did?" a surprised Mando asked.

"*Simón!* I didn't cheat on my tests or nothin'." He then slapped Little Benny's shoulder and said, "I'm glad that we got Latinos taking science classes."

They got back onto their bikes and rode over to the college, which was nearly empty for summer break. The campus was quiet. A sprinkler hissed and turned on a faraway lawn. Someone was playing scales on a piano. A few students milled around the cafeteria and others sat on benches holding open books.

"This is a nice place, homey," Hector said as he scanned the scene. "*La gente* is really good to each other, not pushing nobody to sit at the better benches."

"It ain't like our junior high," Mando agreed. "Where it's always noisy and dirty, huh?"

While Little Benny hurried away to chemistry, Hector and Mando decided to wade in the school fountain. They rolled up their pants legs, got in, and splashed and pushed each other around. They then brought their bikes into the fountain and rode in circles until they were wet and dizzy. After that they sat in the shade. They talked about the worst trouble they had ever gotten into. For Mando it was the time he stamped circles on the dashboard using the cigarette lighter in his dad's car. For Hector it was the time he took the baby-sitter's money from her purse (which he later gave back) after she had been paid. They laughed and rolled in the grass. Mando then said, "Hey, let's go peek in the window and see what Little Benny's doing."

"Good idea," Hector agreed, snapping his fingers and rising to his feet. Grass clippings were stuck to the bottom of his pants. Their tennis shoes squeaked from being drenched in the fountain.

They walked their bikes to the chemistry building, where they forced themselves through scratchy bushes to a window. They cupped their hands around their squinting eyes and looked in, grinning like pumpkins. Little Benny was sitting on a tall stool. He was mixing a blue liquid from a test tube into a tear-shaped bottle. All around him were glass tubes, each one taller than the next, resembling a futuristic city.

"It looks like he's making toilet bowl cleaner," Mando remarked.

"Yeah, it does." Hector agreed. He rapped a knuckle on the window and Little Benny looked up, without expression at first, then horrified to see them there. He waved at them to go away, but to Hector and Mando it looked as if he were waving hello.

"I think he wants us to come in," Hector said.

"Let's go!" Mando shouted.

They hid their bikes in the bushes and hurried to the door. They brushed themselves off, then walked into class. Hector whispered, "Little Benny, it's your *primo*."

The teacher was with a student in the corner of the classroom. He looked up when he heard Hector, but didn't move toward them.

"Little Benny, what are you cooking up?" Hector asked, pointing to a white powder in a beaker. "Looks like you're making pancakes."

"No, I'm testing the acid in these leaves."

"No way! You're pulling our *patas*, our legs," Hector laughed. "You tellin' me that there's acid in 'em?"

The gray-haired teacher approached the boys. A clipboard was pressed under his arm, and his hands were busy with two test tubes.

"You young men must be our guest lecturers," the teacher said brightly. "We've been waiting for you."

Hector looked at Mando, confused. He looked up at the teacher and said, "*Pues*, how long you been waiting, and what for?"

"Weren't you going to share an experiment with us?"

"An experiment?" Hector repeated. His jaw dropped two inches. He felt like the model skeleton in the corner, dead of any kind of meaning.

Mando glanced at Little Benny. He didn't know what to do but for some reason said, "Sure, we can do an experiment. We always like to mix things up."

The teacher walked to the front of the class, clapping his hands and announcing that their visitors from Argentina had arrived.

"Argentina?" Hector said. "Is he *loco o qué*?"

Little Benny lowered his face to Hector's ear and whispered, "Hector, I think he thinks that you're our visitors, two exchange students, from Argentina. He mentioned we were having guests this morning."

"*Híjole*," Hector cried and then broke the news to Mando. "We messed up again, homey."

Head down and worried, Hector walked slowly to the front of the class with Mando in tow. He began to think that maybe the cigarette lighter was nothing compared to the pickle they were in now. He looked around at the faces sizing them up. He felt like an ant.

"Class," the teacher said happily. "Our visitors have arrived — both of them talented young scientists. I believe they're going to show us the experiment that won the International Young Chemists Competition." The teacher smiled at Hector.

Hector took a bow, though no one clapped except Mando, who said, "OK, *carnal*, tell 'em something."

"Be quiet," Hector growled. He made a face at Mando and thought of hitting him, but instead turned to the class of eighteen students, all with combed hair and clean noses. He cleared his throat and said, "I'm here to tell you about salsa. Like the stuff you might put on a taco or an enchilada."

The class looked at him with flat expressions. In the back row, a pencil rolled from the table to the floor.

"OK, here's the deal," Hector continued nevertheless. "Salsa is like a heavy chemistry of this and that. It may look easy to you homeys, but it's the science that makes the tongue happy." He looked around the class. The expressions were still flat as cardboard. "Pull out your *lápices* and take some notes."

The students opened their binders with clicks and clacks and brought out lined paper. This gave Hector time to recall how his grandmother had thrown together the salsa that made his grandfather dance from foot to fiery foot.

"Well, this chemistry is ancient. *Pues*, it's as old as the Aztec calendar, *carnales*, and I'm not talkin' about the calendars in Mexican restaurants. I'm talking about the real one, you know — the round one in stone. So listen up, *vatos*."

He then explained that first you roasted five jalapeño chiles along with three yellow chiles. You usually roasted them in a black pan and then peeled the skin off, but in the lab you could use a Bunsen burner. You next crushed them in a *molcajete*.

"*El molcajete* is like that thing there." Hector pointed to the mortar and pestle on the teacher's desk. He picked up the pestle and began to rotate it like an oar. He began to rattle his mouth. "You guys following? *Entiendes* Mendez? I can't repeat myself, because like the teacher says, we're just visitors — *turistas.*"

The classroom faces now were moving with excitement.

Hector then explained that you thrashed the chiles until their guts spilled seed and the skin disintegrated. Then you tossed this mixture into a larger bowl. Then you added vine-ripe tomatoes if possible, diced onions, a pinch of ground cilantro, and finally some lemon juice.

"Now this is important, *chamacos.*" Hector looked around the room. He saw that they were actually listening. "You remember the song 'Ninety-six Tears'?"

They shook their heads no.

"*Pues*, anyhow, you got to squeeze the lemon ninety-six times. It may take two lemons, but what's important is that you pump the lemon like a rubber ball."

"I thought it was only seventy-six times?" Mando interrupted. His mouth was watering from the recipe.

"No way! I'm talking about my grandmother's recipe which she learned from an *Azteca.* Show some respect."

Just then two boys in eyeglasses appeared at the door, looking like two penguins wearing backpacks. They scanned the classroom. When their gazes locked on the teacher, they announced, "Hello! Have you been expecting us?"

The class turned to the smiling visitors. Hector figured that they were the boys from Argentina.

"*Ay caramba*," Hector said to Mando, who was already sliding up the side of the classroom, ready to make a break for the door if the teacher got mad at them. Then to the class, Hector saluted, "It's nice knowing you, but *mi carnal* and me have to go get a drink of water. All this rapping made us thirsty."

They tiptoed out of the classroom, shame reddening their faces, and looked up to whisper to Little Benny, "We'll be in the cafeteria."

And that's where they went. They bought three sodas — cola, root beer, and orange — and spent the remaining hour experimenting by mixing them up. They burped out new flavors while they waited for their number one *primo*, Little Benny.

CHAPTER 8

On hands and knees, Hector flared his nostrils as he tried to pick up the scent of a water lily. He peered down at the greenish surface of the pond and remarked, "These fish are big as sharks. Do they bite?"

The boys had ridden from Little Benny's house to visit Hector's uncle Isaac in Beverly Hills. Uncle Isaac had showed them the grounds — a gazebo big as a ship, the three swimming pools, the tennis courts, and the six-car garage where a BMW, two Porsches, a classic Cadillac, a Mercedes-Benz, and a meek-looking Miata stared out like caged animals. Now the boys hovered over the kidney-shaped pond, where fish splashed through the surface.

"They're called koi," Uncle Isaac corrected. He was a short man with more hair growing around his ears than on the top of his head. He was Hector's mother's half-brother, a family complication avoided in conversations. He had worked

72

for six years as the chauffeur for Sterling G. Glare, a lawyer for actors and rock stars and, at one time, Spuds McKenzie, the dog who had been in the beer commercials.

"This is a good job," Mando said as he admired the lushness of the yard. "It's like a park but with no litter."

The three stood looking up at the mansion, where Mr. Glare lived with his wife and one daughter, Sarah. Quiet laughter drifted from the balcony, where Mr. Glare was lunching with clients.

"Yes, it is a pleasant place," Uncle sighed, "but there's hardly anything to do."

"Don't you get to drive around Hollywood?" Hector asked. He spat out a cracked sunflower seed, which fell to the ground.

Uncle looked at the shell, then coolly at Hector, who picked it up and stuffed it in his pocket.

"Well, I drive when I'm called upon." He sighed a second time and looked up at the mansion, where the laughter had quieted to a rumble of serious talk and the flash of knives cutting into lunch. He turned to the boys and admitted, "I'm the second chauffeur. My duty is to drive Miss Glare places and, well, entertain her."

"Who's 'Miss Glare'? Sounds like my second-grade teacher," Mando cracked.

"She is — " Uncle started to say.

"I'm Miss Glare," a voice said sharp as a saw. "Sarah Glare, and I want to do something — now."

The three turned and stared, sizing up a girl in a ponytail, hands on hips, the knees of her jeans pale from wear. She was ten years old, and a strawberry birthmark colored her chin. Sarah Glare didn't look friendly. Even the koi fluttered their tails and moved to the other side of the pond.

"Miss Glare, may I introduce my nephew and his very good friend, Armando," Uncle said politely as he took off his chauffeur's cap.

"*Qué pasa*, homegirl?" Mando greeted.

"Pleased to meet you," Hector greeted, extending his hand. She took it and squeezed the color from it, and did the same to Mando's hand.

"You got a good grip," Hector said, shaking out his hand like a rag until a tingle of feeling returned.

"I'm in training," she said with her nose up. "I plan to be in the Olympics one day."

"In what sport?" Hector said.

"In everything."

Hector glanced over to Mando. Neither of them liked her sassiness, and especially didn't like it when she challenged them to an arm-wrestling contest.

"Miss Glare," Hector replied. "You can't beat us homeboys."

She sneered and flexed her arm. A ball of muscle jumped up under her skin, ready for action.

Hector swallowed, truly impressed. He was now full of doubt as she led them to a table under a tree. They sat down and immediately twined their fingers together. She taunted, "Good luck, homeboy." Hector licked his dry lips and was getting ready to reply, "Good luck, rich girl," when she tugged on his hand and the weight of losing bore down on his arm. His arm quivered, but he immediately steadied himself.

This is war, Hector thought. He stared at her hard, blue eyes, and tried to keep from showing his weakness. He kept his breathing shallow and his face flat of emotion. He let her grimace. He let her think that she could beat him, allowing her to move his arm to a 45-degree angle. He even muttered, "You're pretty strong," before he turned on the juice and slammed her hand to the table. She barked out pain and the shame of defeat. No way was Hector going to let her win.

"You're strong yourself," Miss Glare said, mildly impressed, as she worked a sliver from the back of her hand. To Uncle Isaac, she said, "That'll be all for now, Isaac. If you don't mind, I'm going to use your nephews for a couple of hours."

"As you wish, Miss Glare," Uncle Isaac said with a tip of his cap and disappeared into his cabin.

"You don't mind, do you?" Miss Glare asked Hector and Mando. When the boys shook their heads, she said, "Follow me then." She led them to a tennis court, where instead of playing tennis, she handed a bow and a clutch of arrows to Hector. Hector looked at the bow, turning it over and plucking at the taut string.

"Let's have a contest," Miss Glare said as she slipped on a glove. She raised her bow, aimed with one eye scrunched up, and shot at the target, a near bull's-eye. She looked at Hector and yawned, "Your turn."

He turned and faced the target. He looked at Mando, then at Miss Glare, who was peeling off her glove. He looked skyward, where the sun flared behind a stand of eucalyptus. He raised the bow, steadied his aim, and shot. His arrow quivered in the bull's-eye.

Miss Glare looked at Hector, now amazed.

"*Chihuahua*," Mando murmured. "How did you do that, homes?"

"I used to shoot my cats with rubber bands,"

he said loudly and with pride. He handed the bow to Miss Glare and said, "*¿Qué más?*"

"Wait," Mando said. "Let me try a little of this Robin Hood stuff." He took the bow and strummed it like a guitar. When Hector told him to knock it off, he shrugged his shoulders, turned, and winced at the faraway target. He raised the bow and aimed at the target. The arrow whizzed through the trees and disappeared.

"I wonder where it went?" Mando remarked as he stood on tiptoe.

"Never mind the arrow," Miss Glare said coolly. She led them to a covered patio, where there was a Ping-Pong table. She swept off a few leaves from the surface and readjusted the net. She handed a paddle to Hector and asked Mando to shag the balls.

"Hey, I ain't your — what-you-call-it — your butler," Mando snapped back. He spat out a mouthful of sunflower-seed shells and didn't. care where they landed.

Miss Glare scowled at Mando and said, "Very well, then. You can just watch me win."

Hector and Miss Glare rallied slowly at first and then she said, "Let's begin play."

Hector was now determined to win at every game. He didn't like how haughty she was. "You serve, Shorty."

"No, you be my guest," she sneered, the paddle spanking her palm. "And don't call me shorty, Shorty."

Hector served, and they rallied back and forth until Miss Glare caught him off guard with a little dink over the net. With her serve, she rocked on her feet and shot a ball that was so fast Hector couldn't pick it up.

"Very nice," Hector said, twirling his paddle in his hand.

"If that's 'nice,' then this one must be beautiful." She rocked on her toes again as a fiery serve skidded across the table and bounced up, hitting Hector in his Adam's apple.

"Yeah, that was beautiful," he complimented hoarsely. He fought against touching his Adam's apple, which hurt from the sting of the ball.

"It's all in the wrist," she said. "And pushing your weight into the serve."

They rallied back and forth, with Sarah Glare always a point or two ahead. Then Hector went ahead with three dinks himself. Then, a point ahead, he crushed the ball, which skipped across the table and hit Sarah in the Adam's apple. She touched her throat and her eyes brimmed with tears.

"Nice shot," she managed to say. The tears slid down her cheeks, but she refused to wipe them away. One fell on the tabletop.

"If you think that's nice, then the next one is going to be *muy bonita*," Hector taunted mercilessly. He had had enough of her spoiled attitude. He beat Sarah Glare 15–9, and couldn't resist blowing on his paddle like a smoky pistol. When he saw another tear splash on the tabletop, he apologized, "Sorry, Miss Glare. Come on, let's be friends."

She set down her paddle and disappeared into her house.

"Hey, homes, what's wrong with her?" Mando asked. "She got a *muy grande* chip on her shoulder."

"I don't know," Hector said. "She just likes to get her own way, I guess."

They returned to the pond, where they watched the koi and ate sunflower seeds, careful not to spit them on the ground and get Uncle Isaac in trouble. They were arguing about the best football team (for Hector it was the Dallas Cowboys and for Mando it was the Los Angeles Raiders) when a voice said, "All right, let's try a bike race."

The boys turned and stared at Sarah, who had on a helmet, gloves, and a slick outfit that was as bright as a bowl of Fruit Loops. She squeezed her water bottle and a stream arched into her mouth.

"I think we'll just watch the fish," Hector said.

"Me and Mando are kinda tired from our trip."

"What are you, chicken?" she taunted. The birthmark on her face deepened.

"Yeah, kinda, I guess," Hector said with a mouthful of sunflower seeds. Not caring, he spit them on the ground.

"You're scared of a girl beating you?"

"We're shaking," Mando said, shivering his body through pretend chills of fear.

"You're not funny," she snapped.

At this, Hector and Mando turned and stared at the koi until she left. She returned a few minutes later wearing a running outfit.

"How 'bout a race, then? Five miles or ten?"

When Hector shook his head, Sarah stomped away, her running shoes eating up the damp soil. She returned a few minutes later in tennis whites and holding a can of new balls.

"Then how 'bout a game of tennis?" she asked, almost with a begging tone. "I'll even play on my knees."

Hector again shook his head, and again she disappeared only to return wearing a white robe and boxing gloves. "I'm not scared of you! How 'bout ten rounds?"

Hector stood up and suggested, "Let's run backwards around the block, OK?"

"Backwards?" she said, face scrunched up.

"That's what we do in the *barrio*," Hector said.

"We're always running backwards. This way we can see where we been."

"Is that why we do it?" Mando asked, half-serious.

"*Simón, ese.*"

She thought about it for a second. "All right, but let me change first."

She returned wearing her worn jeans and a T-shirt with a baseball cap turned backwards. The three of them went to the front yard, passing the balcony where Mr. Glare's clients were now sipping coffee.

"Which one is your dad?" Hector asked, shading his eyes for a better look.

"The fat bald one," she said without looking up.

Hector and Mando nodded their heads at each other. Now they understood her problem: she didn't like her parents, or at least not her father.

The three lined up on the sidewalk. They agreed that there was no turning around and running forward. As Hector bent down to retie his shoes, Sarah said quickly, "Ready, set, go." Shoes still untied, Hector rose and joined the race, his arms chugging like a locomotive. They chugged, sweated, and at the first corner Hector and Mando sang "I Heard It Through the Grapevine." Sarah told them to be quiet, but they only got louder. On the second corner, while they were singing, "She'll Be Coming Round the Mountain," Hector spotted Mando's lost arrow. It was sticking in a tree.

"¡Mira!" Hector shouted, pointed, and came to a stop.

Mando followed his gaze. "It's my Cupid's arrow."

Sarah slowed down and shouted, "What are you guys doing? You're not quitting, are you?"

"It's Mando's arrow," Hector shouted, pointing. "He wants it for a souvenir."

She joined the boys, running backwards. She gazed upward at the arrow and said, "OK, let's have a contest to see who can climb up and get it first."

Hector and Mando flapped their arms like wings and, worn down by Sarah's endless games, said, "We give up. You win!"

CHAPTER 9

Miss Glare was the first to pull herself limb by limb into the tree and snag the arrow. She was the first to run around the block backwards, the arrow pressed between her arm and chest, quivering and giving the impression that she had been plugged. She felt better after these two wins.

"Good race," she complimented the boys, hands on her knees and breathing hard. She had softened. She had become human, not a dragon with fiery demands. "Let's have dinner together."

That's what they did. She ordered torches set up near the pond and a table with high-back chairs. They feasted on hamburgers and fries, along with milkshakes thick as wet cement. She admitted she didn't like her father because he seldom had time for her. Even then, as they threw their faces into huge burgers, he and her mother were away having dinner with clients.

But she told them she didn't mind, really. This gave her time to work at getting into the Olympics, she reasoned. And over dinner, she invited them — Hector, Mando, and a nervous Uncle Isaac — to a paint-ball war.

"What's that?" Mando asked, lowering a pencil-long French fry into his mouth.

"It's a war game at a special site," she said. "You shoot little balls of paint instead of bullets. It's a lot of fun."

She explained that in a paint-ball war, two enemy teams hunted each other, and the first team to blast all the others won.

"We'll go tomorrow morning," she said. "You guys want to go, don't you?"

"¡Órale!" Hector said. "We want to go, huh, carnal?"

"¡Simón!" Mando agreed. "We're on vacation. Let's live it up before we start school."

Hector felt sorry for her. Her family was distant, not like his own home, which had kids, parents, relatives, neighbors, dogs and cats, even chickens nearly falling out of each open window. It's like Noah's ark, he thought to himself as he pulled a vein of chocolate milk through his straw and into his eager mouth. He felt fortunate coming from such a home.

"You gotta wear old clothes," Sarah said.

"That's easy," Mando joked. "That's all we got, homegirl."

The next morning, the four of them got into the classic Cadillac. With Uncle Isaac at the steering wheel and the three kids in the backseat, they drove through an exclusive area. Sarah pointed out the manicured homes of actors — Julia Roberts, Tom Cruise, Bill Cosby, Roseanne.

"That's where Spuds McKenzie once lived," Sarah pointed. "He had a three-bedroom doghouse that was really cute."

"Shoot," Mando said. "We only got a two-bedroom crib and it ain't pretty at all."

They drove from Beverly Hills toward the industrial side of West Los Angeles. They stopped at a See's Candy Store and bought a five-pound box of assorted chocolates and then stopped at a 7–Eleven to buy bags of sunflower seeds and sodas to wash down the saltiness. While the boys gobbled the chocolates, Sarah cracked sunflower seeds and spat them out the window as the Cadillac sped south along 101 toward Vermont Avenue.

"You're a pro," Hector said of her spitting. "You can hang with the best of us in East Los."

"Miss Glare," Uncle said, looking into the mirror. "May I remind you that you're littering."

"You're right," she said with a thumbs-up

sign, and proceeded to spit shells on the floor of the Cadillac. Once again she explained the rules of paint ball. She told them that they would each get gloves and protective eyewear and a gun that would hold a hundred rounds of paint balls. They would hunt for their enemies and shoot them, in the back if necessary.

"It's like a huge squirt gun, huh?" Mando said. The corners of his mouth were greasy with chocolate.

"*Simón*," Sarah said with laughter.

"*Órale*, girl," Hector laughed. "You're gonna be *gente* in no time."

The three of them shook hands *raza*-style and said that they would protect their gang until the end — or until they ran out of money.

Uncle pulled the boat-like Cadillac onto a street littered with busted mattresses, a bathtub, tattered clothes, and gleaming rivers of broken glass. He parked the car in front of a brick warehouse with a paint-splotched sign that said "Blast of a Time." Two homeless people sat against an abandoned building, their shopping carts weighed down with aluminum cans.

"Miss Glare," Uncle said, "do you think it's wise to park here?"

She looked out the window and scanned the surroundings. "We'll take the chance."

Uncle parked the car, and the three climbed

out, shaking the stiffness from their legs. It had been a long drive on a slow freeway. Uncle hurried them across the street, careful to avoid a man wearing loops of imitation gold chains. "Bargains," the man barked. They waved the man off and entered the warehouse. They walked down a hallway splattered with posters of rock stars and dragsters tearing up the asphalt with their refrigerator-wide tires. At the end of the hallway sat a large man in a Hawaiian shirt. He was eating a cheeseburger and a slice of pizza at the same time.

Wiping his fingers on a napkin, he pointed at four boys. "They're looking for a team to play."

Hector looked at the boys, who stood straight as bowling pins. They were all wearing blue T-shirts that said "Bad."

"You guys want to battle?" Hector asked.

"When you're ready," the tall one said. A smirk was curling up at the corner of his mouth. "We're known as 'bad.' "

"That's 'good,' " Hector smiled. "We're known as 'baddest.' "

When none of them laughed at his joke, Hector shrugged his shoulders and muttered, "I thought it was funny." He brought out some dollar bills from his pocket. Sarah pushed his hand away and said loudly, "No way, I'm paying. You're my guests."

"OK, my treat next," Hector said.

Uncle cleared his throat and said, "Miss Glare, I'll let you and my nephew and Mando enjoy yourselves. Perhaps I have time to polish the car."

"No way," Hector pleaded, pulling on his sleeve. "We need you, Unc."

"Hector, I'm really too old for this." He took off his cap and in the dark hallway of the warehouse, his head shone like a headlight.

"*Tío*, you're not old," Hector countered. "Don't be a *sapo*. Enjoy yourself."

"Isaac," Sarah demanded. "We need you. It's three against four, and we'll lose for sure."

Uncle looked over at the soldiers of Bad and said, "I think we can take 'em."

"All right," Mando said, fist clenched.

They were fitted with eye protection and gloves stiff with dried paint. They were given guns and ammo — a hundred rounds of balls that they pushed into a bottle-like chamber.

"This is crazy," Mando said, cradling his gun. His smile was big enough to pop the chocolate off the corners of his mouth. "I love it!"

They loaded their paint guns and the man in the Hawaiian shirt licked the burger grease off his fingers and led everyone into the main part of the warehouse, which was dark and almost airless. An overhead fan droned, but still the dampness was thick. In the corner a Coke machine hummed.

The pimply leader of Bad said, "Give us two minutes to hide, and you come and look for us."

"We'll give you three," Hector said, then added, "and we'll give you some chocolates for energy. This may be your last meal, dude." He tugged the box from the reluctant Mando and opened the lid. The perfume of chocolate wafted in the air. With dirty fingers, the Bad soldiers groped for the best ones, and then the boys took off to go hide. Hector noticed that the leader wore heavy boots, while the others were quiet as cats in their dirty tennies.

The "war front," as it was called, was three levels of floor. There were boxes, bolted walls, and cardboard barrels to hide behind. There were hallways and a maze of corners in which to avoid the blast of the balls. There were shadows and dark patches where an enemy could also hide.

"I feel ridiculous," Uncle said, holding the gun against his palm. His breathing had fogged his eyewear.

"Unc, you look great in those glasses," Hector argued.

"Yeah, you're smooth, *hombre*," Mando agreed. "Like one of those *vatos* from *Star Trek*."

They jumped when a voice said, "We're

ready," and a single blast thudded on the wall above their heads. They ducked and rolled. Hector fired his paint gun at the dark, getting a bead on a soldier of Bad. He missed, and then missed again when he saw a belt buckle wink for a second. He blasted a burst of rounds, the paint gun jerking against his shoulder.

"I'm going over there," Sarah whispered, jerking her chin. She scooted her body toward a wall, skipping over a blast of a paint ball.

"Missed, dude," she laughed.

"But I put fear in your life," he taunted back.

She crouched and fired six rounds when a member of Bad tried to leap over a barrel to a box. He took the shots in three places — shoulder, hip, and *nalgas*.

"I'm out!" he yelled, raising his gun in surrender and rubbing his butt. He left the war front, jumped over the wall that was the "out" area, and sat on a bench near the Coke machine. He pulled out a bag of Chee·tos and watched the war.

Hector and Mando advanced toward a wall, and then called, "Uncle, come on."

"I'm really against such violence," he cried. "I protested the Vietnam War."

Uncle then spotted an enemy on the third level. He stood, legs splayed and teeth gritted, and fired twenty rounds. He missed by a mile, then took a shot on the top of his bald head. He was out, paint dripping on his head like a broken egg. He joined the boy on the bench and shook his head when the boy offered a peace pipe in the form of Chee·tos.

Mando fired a round at an enemy on the second floor. The enemy fired back, which had Mando dancing.

"I was doing the Mexican hat dance, *carnal*," Mando said after the rounds had stopped. "He almost wiped me out, man."

"Be careful!" Hector advised as he rose from his knees. "Cover me."

With Mando's gun raised in protection, Hector ran toward the stairway, his heart jumping like a frog beneath his shirt. He peered up the stairway, then pulled his head back when he saw a barrel pointing at him. Two rounds whizzed by his face. The paint ran like blood on the floor.

"*Chihuahua*," he whistled. He looked back up the stairway. The enemy had disappeared like smoke.

He heard the sound of boots start and stop. The sound was echoing on the third level. He moved quickly up the steps and onto the second floor, where he immediately rolled when he saw an enemy run around a corner. The enemy showed his head, then pulled it back.

"Go ahead, *vato*, make my day," Hector muttered to himself. He timed the head that kept swinging into view, then out of view, then back into view. On the fourth swing, Hector came up firing. The paint balls slapped the enemy three times in the face.

"I'm hit! Enough!" the enemy cried with his rifle raised in surrender. He walked down the steps, past Mando and Sarah who were running up the stairs, and joined Uncle and the other boy on the bench.

"Two down and two bad dudes to go," Hector said.

"Where are the other dudes?" Mando asked.

A round of blasts whizzed by their heads, and they all jumped halfway down the stairs.

"Up there, to answer your question," Sarah said. She shot toward the third floor and then advanced among a splatter of shots.

"I'm gonna check out the other side," Mando said and turned. He took two steps, looked up, and felt a single shot in the belly from a sniper hiding behind a barrel. He touched his belly and groaned, "Bad luck! They got me, homes. Send a letter to my momma." He hurried away, head down, disgusted with himself for getting tagged.

The sniper fired again, this time at Hector. The paint balls skidded at his feet, and one splattered near his ear. They fired back, and the fat-boy enemy hopped away. Hector leaped down the steps and into a roll as round as a doughnut. He came up firing and his enemy took a shot in the back and one in the leg.

"*¡Órale!*" Mando yelled like a cheerleader. His face was fat with Chee·tos.

Hector was smiling when he took a shot in the back of the neck, a hard thud that had him rolling again. He was out and mad at himself. He lay there for a second, breathing hard, then rose to his feet. "Good shot, dude," he yelled and sat down on the bench.

"This is sweet, huh?" Mando exclaimed. "It's better than dirt clods, like back in our *barrio*."

"Yeah, this is bad," Hector said. He looked toward the third floor. In the dim light, he could make out the leader of Bad moving toward Sarah, whose back was to him. He wanted to yell, "Watch out, homegirl," but kept his mouth closed. His heart thumped and sweat filled the lines on his palms. He knew that Sarah wanted to win and scratch another notch on her bedpost.

"Turn, Sarah," he said to himself as the leader raised his gun. "He's on you."

Sarah dropped when she heard his boot bump against a wall. She scooted into a dark patch of nothingness. The leader fired and looked around in bewilderment. His target was gone. He took a noisy step and fired again at a handful of sunflower seeds that Sarah threw out to distract him.

The leader turned and shot at the seeds. His back was now her target. She didn't think twice. Five paint balls riddled the back of his legs and then his throat when he turned in surprise, a moan of defeat gurgling out the words, "You got me, girl."

CHAPTER 10

"We're leaving today for *Tía's* house," Hector told his mom. They were speaking by telephone on a Thursday morning, seven days into Hector and Mando's journey. Hector heard the shuffling of playing cards, and he asked, "Did you already go to Las Vegas?"

"*Pues sí,*" his mother said, shuffling the cards again.

He had to smile when he pictured his mother. She was probably at the kitchen table, her hair rolled in her favorite blue curlers, scanning the newspaper for weekend yard sales. "Did you win?"

"No, but I got some ashtrays that they gave away, and some really pretty drinking glasses."

Hector said that his stay at Uncle Isaac's was fun. He told her about Sarah, who had invited the boys to eat a fancy dinner with her parents the night before.

"You should have seen it, Mom," Hector said. "There was grub for days."

The grub had been lobster, a potato soufflé, almond rice, salade Niçoise, and a circle of snails in garlic butter. The last dish Hector and Mando only looked at and rolled around their plates, hoping that the twirl of their forks would make the snails disappear. They didn't. Nearly crying, they put them in their mouths and washed them down with Cidre Mousseux, apple cider. Just as it had been at Bentley's there were two spoons, two forks, two knives, and only one napkin, a mistake because the boys needed at least two. Instead, they rolled their tongues around their sticky mouths.

"Did you call your *tía*?" his mother asked. Her shuffling had stopped. Her speech was now a mumbling from a bite of doughnut, a mumbling that was followed by a smack of lips and a swallow of coffee.

"Yes. She said she's expecting us. She said she's gonna take us to some kind of art show."

His mother told him to be good, to not get hurt, and to thank his uncle Isaac. While talking man-to-man, his uncle Isaac had told them that he and his sister — Hector's mom — had had a falling out. He was the older brother from their father's first marriage. Their family history was filled with bickering and hurt feelings.

"Do you wanna talk to Uncle?" Hector asked. "He wants to talk to you, Mom."

"He does?"

"Yeah."

There was silence on her end. Then she said, "Just tell him that we're gonna have a really good barbecue in a couple of weeks."

After listening to a hundred warnings to be careful, Hector hung up, and yelled, "Mando! Let's go, homes."

Mando came into Uncle's small living room with a pile of newly washed clothes.

"Check it out, homes," Mando said, putting his face into the sweet smells of clean socks and *chones*. "Sarah's maid washed the stink out of our clothes."

They stuffed the clothes into their backpacks and led their bikes down the path toward the front of the mansion where Sarah sat, her left shoe on her right foot.

"Hey, why don't we have a race with our shoes on backwards?" Sarah suggested. Her look was desperate. She had spent two days running the boys ragged. They played tennis, and Sarah won, nearly stuffing the furry balls down their throats with her ace serves. They played racquetball at a country club and swam the 500 meters. Again she won and won and won at every game. This made Hector think that maybe, just maybe, Sarah could make the cut for the Olympics.

"Sarah, we gotta go," Hector said. "We really enjoyed our stay." He raised his arm and made a muscle. "See, I even got stronger working out with you."

"Just one more contest," she pleaded.

"No, Sarah, really. You're the champ and we're the chumps."

Sarah looked down at her shoes, and for a moment Hector thought she was going to cry. When she looked up her eyes were shiny. She smiled and said, "OK, dudes. I'll catch up with you one day, maybe at the beach."

"Don't be mad at us," Hector said.

"I'm not," she said simply, chewing on her bottom lip.

They said their good-byes. They shook hands with Uncle Isaac, who stood by the gleaming Cadillac, a towel over his sleeve and a can of polish in his hands.

The boys pushed off waving their good-byes and smiling big, but not so big that they would swallow a gnat. It had been a good stopover, a rich fill of food, games, and great sleep in Sarah's spare bedroom. Hector now knew how the rich lived: they lived very well, but like most families they had their troubles. But he figured that Sarah would do well, in spite of her anger that her parents never spent time with her. Before he met her, he wouldn't have felt sorry for anyone with three pools and two tennis courts and more money than the leaves on a tree. Now he did. Hector looked back at Sarah, a small figure waving good-bye.

They rode south toward West Hollywood, a ten-mile ride, and instead of going directly to *Tía*'s they decided to stop at the Hollywood Wax Museum.

"We got nearly eighty bucks," Hector said when Mando asked if they could afford the admission. "And we don't have to eat 'til dinnertime, the way we grubbed this morning."

They rode and rode and when they finally arrived at the museum, they were hot as candles and angry at the thousand and one motorists who had honked at them. They locked up their bikes, shrugged their backpacks onto their shoulders, and approached the ticket booth. They crouched a little bit, said that they were eleven years old, and the bored cashier poked a finger at a red button and the machine spit out two tickets for $6.95 each.

"It's nice and cool in here," Hector remarked, yanking at his collar as heat billowed up from his sticky clothes. He was sweaty and thirsty. He drank at the water fountain, filling up like a camel. Then Hector and Mando checked their backpacks at security. They started their tour.

"*Mira*, it's Clint Eastwood," Mando yelled. They hurried over to stand in front of cowboy Clint Eastwood, his lined face scowling. They slurred in unison, "Go ahead, *vato*, make my day."

They moved to Hulk Hogan, the bad-boy wrestler, and they puffed up their bony chests. They threw punches at Joe Louis and strummed air guitars when they came across The Beatles. They yawned at Jane Fonda and Clark Gable, and laughed at Popeye and Olive Oyl. They wished they had a big sister like Wonder Woman, who they figured could help them with their homework and fights at school. They weren't sure about Frank Sinatra.

"I heard of the dude," Hector said, stumped about who he was.

"Me, too. I think maybe he was a politician, *qué no?*"

But they had heard of Elvis. Hector owned a yard-sale album of his golden hits, and his mom even had a cigarette lighter that was a statue of Elvis — a flame leaped up from his black hair.

"There's The King," Mando said, jerking his chin at a slim and young-looking Elvis Presley with his sneering mouth.

Both of them liked to read about The King in the tabloids at the checkout stands. Elvis was appearing all over the world. He had been reported buying groceries in Pomona, and had been sighted getting into a truck in Ontario. Someone had seen him fishing in Big Bear and others had seen him drinking a Big Gulp at a destruction derby in Tarzana.

"You think he's alive?" Mando asked.

"Nah, man, this is a wax statue," Hector said.

"No, dude. I mean people think he's still living and planning for a big comeback."

"Yeah, maybe." Hector looked at Elvis and then said, "I'd like to see him in concert."

"I'm sure he wouldn't mind seeing himself in concert," Mando said matter-of-factly. They walked from room to room and were soon bored. The statues seemed fake to them.

Hector then turned, snapped his fingers, and said, "Hey, let's pretend we're wax statues."

Mando's eyes sparkled at the idea. "Who we gonna be?"

"I don't know. Let's go over and stand by Popeye." He looked down at his clothes. "Who's famous in T-shirts and jeans?"

"No one. But who cares. Let's give it a try, dude."

There was a roped-off, raised platform with an overhead light. The boys climbed over the rope, careful not to be seen by security. They decided to stand frozen and see what people thought. They stood facing each other, shaking hands.

They didn't wait long. A baby with two teeth came tottering by, pointing and muttering, "Popeye, Popeye." He had on a baseball cap that said, "Make My Day." The baby turned and cooed in a squeaky voice, "Nice boys. Friends."

Hector wanted to laugh. His shoulders were jerking up and down and his closed mouth was holding back a stream of laughter. The baby climbed the platform, tottered, and walked behind Mando. The baby repeated, "Friends," and wiped his sticky fingers on Mando's pants. Eyes wide and joking, Mando raised a hand, as if to spank the baby.

The baby came down from the platform when he heard his name.

"That little dude," Mando whispered as he

stood frozen. "He thinks I'm a paper towel or something."

"¡Cállate!" Hector scolded. "Here come some turistas."

A family of three approached Popeye and Olive Oyl. They were French and loaded with cameras. They took a picture of Popeye, and then moved a few feet to view Hector and Mando.

"Who are these boys?" the mother asked, searching for the placard that would tell them about their fame. "Who are these boys?"

"American boy actors," the girl said. "I think they were in the movie *Home Alone*." She was about their age, but taller and smartly dressed in a white blouse and designer jeans. The daughter added, "He looks cute," referring to Hector.

Hector nearly laughed and, looking at Mando, he could see a smirk pulling at the corners of his mouth.

"They look real," the father said. He took the lens cover off his camera and began shooting.

Hector was now worried. A fly had settled on his forehead and was cruising in low-gear around his face. It crawled from his forehead to his cheek and then jumped to his nose, where it hunkered. Hector looked cross-eyed at the fly. He shot a quick breeze of nostril air, and the fly jumped to Mando's face, where it took a lap around his mouth. Mando wiggled his mouth, but the fly still clung stubbornly. Hector could see that Mando wanted to sneeze but was holding back. He could even feel a trembling in their handshake. His palm was dripping with sweat.

The French tourists took a few more pictures, and as they wandered lazily away, Mando sneezed. The father turned and said, "Bless you." He did a double take and began to speak rapidly and shake his head as they moved on to the next wax statue.

When they were out of view, the boys climbed off the platform, cursing the fly. They rotated their stiff necks. They hurried for the exit, then skidded in their tracks when they remembered their backpacks.

"And did you hear that girl say that you were so cute?"

"It's true."

"Man, you're living in a dream world," Mando laughed. "Then that little diaper dude wiping his dirty hands on *mis pantalones*." He looked down at his pants. They still seemed clean but were wrinkled from pumping the bike.

They had had enough of the Hollywood Wax Museum. They had had enough of standing frozen on a platform and pretending they were famous people. They left the building, the brightness of the day hurting their eyes. It took a minute for their eyes to adjust. When they opened them, the French family was staring at them. The bewildered father again removed the lens cap of his camera, and the girl said in English, "There they are! The famous American movie stars!"

The boys hurried for their bikes, unlocked them, and rode as fast as they could to get away from the embarrassment that clung to their faces.

CHAPTER 11

Hector and Mando fled the Hollywood Wax Museum and rode around Hollywood Boulevard looking at weird people. The most average person they saw was a guy with purple hair and a safety pin hooked in his nose. The rest were spaced out, they concluded, including one member of *la raza*, a dude playing an air guitar to the classical music of his radio.

"Poor guy," Hector whispered to Mando, who nodded his head in agreement.

They went into a record store and for an hour flipped through the CDs, constantly followed and eyed by security. Not feeling welcome, they left.

"Come on," Hector growled as he pushed through the turnstile. "Let's take our money somewhere else!"

"Yeah, let's go buy some doughnuts."

They left the record store, surprised that dusk had settled and that the traffic lights were bright

against the backdrop of the L.A. sky. They un-
chained their bikes, crossed the street, and
bought three doughnuts each, which they
washed down with a carton of milk. While they
were licking their fingers, Hector suggested
that they visit Grauman's Chinese Theatre, the
place where the actors had their handprints
pressed in cement. They figured they could look
at the handprints and then look at more weird
people.

"Yeah, I want to check out Hercules' handprints," Mando said.

"Man, Hercules ain't got his prints there,"
Hector said, crushing his milk carton.

"That's what my uncle says," Mando retorted.

"You're playing with me." Hector turned and
tossed his crushed milk carton at a garbage can
and missed. He picked it up again and at close
range made it with a hook shot.

They got on their bikes and rode toward
Grauman's Chinese Theatre. After two miles
up streets, down alleys, and through vacant lots
they were lost. They stopped a Mexican woman
with three children and asked directions in
Spanish. She thought they were asking where
Chinatown was and pointed in the wrong
direction.

"*Gracias,*" Hector said and, popping a wheelie,
took off north on Vine Street with Mando in hot

pursuit. They rode in silence and soon the bright lights of Hollywood gave way to darkness and a river of glass that shone under their bike tires. The boys skidded to a halt.

"Hey, man," Hector said, breathing hard. "I think the lady gave us the wrong direction."

"I think so." Mando looked up at a building that was gutted by fire. The windows were blown out and black soot smothered the outside. In front of the building two smashed cars hunkered with their tires gone. Even the windshields were gone and the antennae were looped into question marks.

They walked their bikes through the blighted area and when a man in mummy-like rags approached them asking for money, whining that he needed two quarters for coffee, they hopped on the bikes and sped away, scared and perspiring under their clothes. They rode in circles, lost and now worried.

"Let me call my *tía*," Hector told Mando. "You got a quarter?"

Mando patted his pants pocket and pulled out a wad of crumpled one-dollar bills, a nickel, two bright pennies, and a crushed Life Saver that formed the letter "C." He shook his head and said, "Nah."

The area was bombed out and gutted of hope. A group of men sat on the steps of an abandoned house, drinking from paper bags. One stood up and said, "Hey, kids, we need your help."

Hector and Mando rode away, not looking back. They rode to a liquor store, where the clerk refused to give them change unless they made a purchase. They bought a bag of sunflower seeds.

"That's cold," Mando complained. "He could have given us change."

They went outside, muttering under their breath.

"Come, let's call my *tía* to come and pick us up," Hector said, pointing with his chin at the telephone booth, slashed with graffiti.

Hector dropped a quarter into the slot of the telephone and was about to deposit an additional thirty-five cents when three crazy dudes jumped them from behind. One guy ripped the phone from Hector's hands and another pushed his finger into the change return.

"*Nada,*" he snarled. "Come, let's jack 'em up."

They dragged them, bikes and all, into the shadows, yelling at them to close their eyes or else. The *vatos* pressed their faces toward a brick wall.

"Hey, dudes," Hector cried, peeking between his fluttering eyelashes. His heart pounded and sweat flooded his armpits. "We didn't do anything to you."

"Shaddup," growled one, wearing a Raiders baseball cap turned backward. The tattooed heart on his forearm began to pulsate from anger. "Puppet, check his pants."

"Puppet!" Mando screamed, eyes open and big as hubcaps. He remembered his cousin Larry Delgado whose running name in the street was Puppet. He hadn't seen him in the six years since Puppet had moved from East Los Angeles to the traffic-clotted heart of Los Angeles — Echo Park. "It's me, *su primo!*"

"Yeah, sure, you *cholito,*" Puppet growled as he pushed his hands into Mando's pockets and brought out a wad of dollar bills and the cracked Life Saver. He turned the candy over in his hands and then tossed it in his mouth.

"It's me — Mando."

Puppet was the tallest of three and the strongest, his arms hard as baseball bats. His front tooth was chipped and already a worry line snaked across his brow. He turned Mando around and looked at him, his breath hot and smelling of sunflower seeds. He gave him a curious look and then asked, "OK, man, if you're *mi primo*, then tell me my momma's name."

"Claudia," Mando answered. "But they call her 'Baby.' "

A smile cut across Puppet's face as he slapped

Mando in his arm and pulled the fat of his cheek. "You're not the little dude from East Los?"

"Yeah, that's me," Mando beamed.

"The one we put in the dryer and spun around?"

"Yeah, that's me, Puppet." Mando touched the top of his head and then taking Puppet's hand, said, "Here, feel it, bro'."

Puppet felt the knot and then cooed, "*Carnal*, long time no see."

"Yeah, long time. Since I just got off my bike with training wheels."

"What are you *vatos* doing around here? It's a dangerous place, even for us." Puppet gazed around the rundown area, where every house had windows with bars and huge lights shone on oily driveways.

"Where are we?" Mando asked.

"Near Echo Park, homey."

"*Híjole*," Mando said, shaking his head. "We're trying to go over to the Chinese theater to check out the handprints."

"Dudes, you're way off." Puppet looked at Hector and asked, "Who's your sidekick?"

"This is Hector. Me and him are on this bike ride, sort of like on a vacation. We're visiting all of Hector's relatives."

"Shoot, I'm a relative. Let's go to my crib,"

Puppet said after he pounded his palm into Hector's shoulder, an act of friendship. "But let me first introduce you to my homeys — Ángel and Lalo."

They shook hands with Puppet's homeys, who handed back their money, backpacks, and bikes.

"Now say you're sorry for jumping *mi primo*," Puppet joked with a straight face.

"We're sorry," both boys chimed like choirboys with big toothy smiles.

Hector returned to the liquor store and bought sodas, Sno Balls, and sunflower seeds for everyone. They then headed toward Puppet's house, this time not sneaking in the shadows but out in the middle of the street chattering up a good time.

"So, what's been happening, Mando?" Puppet asked.

"Just school."

"Your *familia* doing OK?"

"*¡Simón!* My dad's on the late shift at Anheuser-Busch."

"Hey, man, he gets to sleep at work and gets free beer."

Puppet's two running mates said they had to take off. The beeper on Lalo's belt buzzed and he knew it was time to get home or answer to his father. They watched them hustle away until they were eaten up by the darkness of the streets.

"They're good dudes," Puppet crowed. "Loyal."

"Where did you meet 'em?" Hector asked.

"In juvie. We got snagged stealing some bikes from K Mart."

Hector swallowed hard and looked down at his chrome handlebars. He smiled at Puppet, trying to keep on his good side.

At Puppet's house, they sat on the front porch under the yellow haze of the porch light. A moth banged at the bulb and the boys tapped their feet to the Chicano radio program called *The Sancho Show*. Sancho was playing "Ninety-six Tears" when the telephone rang, and Puppet sprang to his feet and hurried into the house. "OK, be right there," he yelled into the phone. He came out onto the porch and said, "It's bingo time."

The call was from his mother, who had instructed Puppet to look in the freezer for a ten-dollar bill wrapped in aluminum foil for safe keeping. He went over to the refrigerator, which he opened with a screwdriver because the handle was broken. He got the bill from underneath a pound of brick-hard hamburger and they took off to play bingo at St. Joseph's church.

The boys hurried to the church and descended the stairs into the basement where a stratum of cigarette smoke hovered near the ceiling. The basement was crowded with players, young and old, grumbling over their cards. A woman was up at a podium calling, "G-19," which started more grumbling.

Hector eyeballed the scene. His mom had taken him twice to a bingo game and twice he won prizes: once a box of Baby Ruth candy bars and the other time an inflatable Barney doll, which he used as his punching bag when he started taking karate lessons.

"Let's play," Hector said, rubbing his palms together in the friction of excitement.

"I ain't got nothing except what I was gonna steal from you two jokers," Puppet laughed.

"That's no problem, *primo*," Mando said. He pushed his hands into his pocket and brought out the wad of dollar bills. He slapped three into Puppet's outstretched palms. Puppet closed his fist on the bills and said, "*Órale.* Let's get down and play, homeys."

But before they took a step, they heard a voice cry across the room, "Puppet! *¡Ándale!*"

They looked up — Puppet's mom was wiggling her long, manicured fingernails at them.

"It's my mom," Puppet said. "Your *tía*."

The last time Mando had seen his aunt she was slim as a tulip, and now she was thick as a cement truck. Her hair then was black and now it was orange. Cheap bracelets chimed a tinny music from her sausage-like wrists.

"I better say hi," Mando said as he started to work his way through the aisle crowded with players sitting in folding chairs. Most were smoking and others were dipping doughnuts into their coffee.

"Mom, guess who this dude is," Puppet yelled over the noise as they approached his mother.

"One of your *cholo* friends," his mother answered hotly. She snatched the ten-dollar bill and looked down at her card when "G-10" was called.

"Nah, mom, he's your nephew," Puppet said. "You know, Uncle Trini's boy."

His mother gazed up with a puzzled look on her face. She eyed him hard through her bluish eyeliner and then asked him to step closer. She felt the knot on the top of his head, clapped her hands together and laughed, "You *are* Trini's boy! The one Puppet put in the dryer."

"That's me," Mando beamed, the knot on his head pulsating with pride.

She gave him a hug and a pat on the head. She asked about his family but snapped a hard stare at her card when "O-7" was called. She stomped her foot and said, "Oh, shoot." Then she looked up again, smiling so wide that the boys could see her chewing gum curled up nicely on the back of her molars. She was asking about his family when "B-4" was called. Snapping a desperate look at her card, she whined, once again stomped her foot, and said, "Shoot." She sighed. She again looked up, took a swig from her Styrofoam coffee cup, and asked about the family. Before he could answer, a woman in white gloves yelled, "Bingo!" The crowd moaned. Puppet's mother stomped her feet and pounded her fist on the table.

The boys left Puppet's mother and walked over to the bin where the bingo cards were piled. They were a dollar each or five for three dollars.

Hector pushed his hands into his pockets and brought out a ten-dollar bill. "I'm going for it," he told Mando and Puppet, who slapped his shoulders and crowed, "Go, homey!"

The big prize for the evening was a bicycle. Hector figured that if he won he could give it to Puppet for a present and keep him off the street and from bothering little kids. He bought fifteen bingo cards and with the help of Mando and Puppet played them in a far corner on a wobbly table. They played all night and when the big prize came around, Hector bought three more cards.

The three boys felt like stockbrokers, their eyes and hands moving over the cards. No one was much interested in the bike. Most of the bingo players wanted toasters or vacuum cleaners or the bus tickets to Las Vegas, a bingo player's paradise. The boys played their cards and though they had eighteen cards altogether, they lost and stomped their feet. They lost to Puppet's mother, who stood up, bracelets jangling on her wrists. She screamed so loud that their wobbly table collapsed, scattering the cards.

Still, it was a winning night. Puppet's mother gave the bike to her son and Mando gave all his cards to his *tía*. The boys took the bike up the steps and with Hector on the handlebars and Mando on the crossbar, Puppet pushed off. The boys rode out into the dark, winners on a hot night of church bingo.

CHAPTER 12

Puppet gained a new bicycle and Hector and Mando gained a well-deserved sleep on Puppet's waterbed. They rose near noon and, in a hurry, hopped onto their bikes. Two hours later they arrived at their next stop—Aunt Teresa's house. But during their bike ride, they held a one-on-one wheelie contest. They popped their bikes and rode like circus monkeys. They apologized for nearly hitting a lady's cart and sped away. And they raced from dogs that chased them, dogs whose teeth were crooked as dice and yellow as weeds. They raced away from two other boys, both older and wearing red bandannas, a bad sign as far as they were concerned. The boys told them to get out of their *barrio*.

"*Tía*," Hector called from behind a three-foot-high chain-link fence. Behind the fence stood a small, white house with a cement porch and flowers by the boatload. A small Mexican flag decal clung to the window. Hector opened the gate and walked his bike in, followed by Mando, who closed the gate and asked, "She doesn't have a dog, does she?"

"I don't think so."

He looked at the slip of paper scribbled with her address.

"What does she do?" Mando asked.

"She teaches kindergarten."

"My best subject. Coloring."

"Auntie," he called again. "It's me and Mando."

"*Come here, chamacos,*" they heard a voice say. They looked around. They didn't see anyone and jumped when they heard, "Get over here and help me, you rascals!" To Hector, the voice sounded just like his mom's and just as loud. But the voice belonged to his mom's younger sister, Teresa. She came from the garage, carrying buckets of paint. She was dressed in a white Mexican dress, earrings that chimed, jangling bracelets, and white sandals. She put down the buckets, smiled at the boys, and then scolded, "Where have you been? I was expecting you a long time ago."

"At the Hollywood Wax Museum, *Tía,*" Hector explained, trying to look innocent. "You look really pretty."

"Thank you, *mi'jo.*" She have him a kiss and asked, "Who's this handsome fellow?"

"Where? I don't see anyone handsome," Hector answered with a smirk on his face.

"She means me," Mando said, playfully shoving his friend.

"You?" He introduced Mando, who said that he'd heard she taught kindergarten.

"I learned to tie my shoes in kindergarten," Mando told her. "That's where I learned to scribble on my bedroom wall, too." He told her that red was his favorite color for painting.

Hector gave Mando a funny look. Smiling, *Tía* looked at the twin buckets of paint. "Actually, this paint is for you knuckleheads." She pulled her hair back behind her ears, bracelets jangling like wind chimes.

"What do we have to paint, Auntie?" Hector looked at her house, which was white and done up with flowers. "Looks cool to me."

"No, I'll explain a little later."

The boys helped Hector's aunt haul buckets of sloshing paint into her VW van, a battered vehicle with a drooping headlight. They stored their bikes in the garage and followed Aunt Teresa into her house. They unpacked, washed up, and pigged out on some *chicharrones* and cream soda. They burped and felt better, smacking their lips. While Hector's aunt was on the telephone, the boys wandered around her house, curious as two kittens. They liked the house, which was a jungle of potted plants and loops of incense smoke burning under a poster of Carlos Santana. There was a picture of Cesar Chávez, a statue of the Virgin of Guadalupe, wooden animals from Mexico, a calendar of an Aztec warrior cuddling his girlfriend, a hand-made *serape*, and a mirror with a tin frame. Hector smiled into the mirror and scraped a lot of *chicharrones* from his front teeth.

Next, Mando stood in front of the mirror, combing his hair with his fingers. He smiled and blew a kiss. Hector crowded in. He shoved Mando away and filled the reflection with a wide grin and a smacking kiss. Mando then shoved Hector from the mirror.

After his aunt got off the telephone, Hector asked, "Where we going, *Tía*?"

"To an art opening," his aunt answered as she hurried to the kitchen, pushing her way through a bead curtain. She got her purse and keys and lifted the head of a pig cookie jar, pulling out a twenty-dollar bill.

"What's an art opening?" Hector asked as he was shoved by Mando. Hector let Mando have the mirror. Mando again smiled. He stood so close to the mirror that his breathing fogged the surface.

"It's when an artist shows his or her work at a gallery." She grinned at the two of them mugging in the mirror. She thought Hector was the spitting image of his mother. "OK, you boys, stop fooling around and let's get in the van."

They locked up, leaving the porch light on. They got into the van and rattled away, the motor backfiring and rumbling a dark, stinky smoke. They got onto Freeway 101, then Freeway 10. To Hector's surprise, the old van kept up with the flow of traffic. "Do you know this artist?"

"Yes. He's a friend."

"You mean, a boyfriend, huh, Auntie?" Hector asked with a sly look. He believed that when you reached age thirty, romance was over.

"*Chale.* He's just a guy. But I am looking around." She changed lanes, her bracelets jangling like music, and winked at Hector. "Do you have a *novia*?"

Hector clammed up. He didn't have a girlfriend.

"Where's this place?" Hector asked after a while.

"Actually, it's near your house. It's called Self-Help Graphics."

"It is?" Hector asked with surprise. He looked out the window. We're heading east, all right, he thought to himself.

"*Chihuahua,*" Mando whistled. "I hope Mom doesn't see me."

Hector had to laugh. They had been bicycling for six days, moving from relative to relative, and now they were back where they started. The *barrio* wouldn't let them go, even though they wouldn't be ready to return until they'd made it to Santa Monica.

His aunt pulled off the freeway and landmarks became identifiable. There were familiar stores, the playground where they had had their faces painted, their old elementary school, Mexican music floating from bars, the "roach coaches" serving tacos and huge burritos — the evidence that they were near home.

"Do you want to stop at your house? Hector? Mando?"

"No," both screamed.

Hector looked at Mando and Mando looked out the window, pointed, and said, "I only live three blocks from here."

"You don't want to see your parents?" Auntie repeated, playing with the boys. "I'm sure they miss you so much."

"No," Mando said with a snap in his voice. "They'll probably make me mow the lawn or wash the car or something."

Aunt Teresa laughed and shifted down as they pulled onto Highland Avenue and started up past the Chinese cemetery where Hector and Mando had made up their ghost story. They arrived at Self-Help Graphics, the Chicano Art Museum. They pushed their way through the crowd celebrating the prints and paintings of Gronk, a Chicano artist and Auntie Teresa's friend. They kissed and hugged.

"This *chavalo* is my nephew," Auntie said with a wave of her hand. "And this is his friend Mando. They're staying with me."

They shook hands. Gronk asked their ages and where they lived. Hector told him around the corner and then tried to explain that they were on a bike trip. Gronk looked at the boys, trying to size up their story.

"Wear white at night," he advised.

They parted when Gronk heard his name called and the handshakes and hugging began with a new group of people.

"This is pretty nice stuff," Hector crowed, standing in front of a painting of a woman with big red lips. They smacked their own lips when they eyed two platters of food. They weren't sure if they could help themselves, but then they saw everyone else sawing away at the carrots, radishes, midget pickles, and crackers smeared with cheese. They moved in to help themselves to the finger food and the icy mineral water. They hoarded their food on paper plates and then wandered around the art gallery. They saw everything in five minutes.

"I bet you he's a millionaire," Mando remarked, wagging his head. A carrot stick was sticking out of his mouth like a cigarette.

"*Simón*. Chicano artists are the best." In front of a painting of a woman holding a smiling skull, Hector added, "Shoot, I should have saved my artwork from kindergarten. I'd be rich."

"Let's get out of here," Mando said as he was squeezed between two viewers. "This place is packed."

They left the art gallery, seeking fresh air and room to flap their elbows. They finished their mineral water and burped simultaneously.

"Let's go for a walk," Hector suggested. "My aunt is going to be there for days."

"*Vámonos*."

Without noticing, the boys started walking in the direction of Hector's house. In the afternoon dusk, they walked in silence, kicking cans and chunks of asphalt. They talked about the Los Angeles Dodgers and how lucky they were to bag a luxury box. They talked about Sarah, whom they liked for her gutsiness, and poor Uncle Ricky, for whom they wished wealth and a hit song from Chilly Lagoon. They were talking about science-brain Bentley when a German shepherd began to bark at them from behind a chain-link fence. The boys barked back, taunting the dog.

"Come on, *perrito*, make my day," Mando yelled.

The riled dog jumped the fence and started chasing them, trying to do just that.

"Be cool, dog," Mando huffed. "Dogs are our favorite animals. *De veras*."

Hector looked back. The dog with the flapping tongue was looking directly at him, and he was sure it was thinking, "I'm going to make dinner out of your legs." The dog chased them two blocks until they were on Hector's own street and the dog had given up, turning around with a flip of his tail.

"Hey, man, we're close to my house," Hector said, looking around like a gopher from its hole. He was closer than he thought: within shouting distance of his mother, who was talking with *Señora* Lopez. They were on *la señora*'s porch where rumors — *chisme* — were verified, weighed, and spread like seed. The two women were chewing on gossip.

The boys crouched behind a car, letting the sweat drain over their bodies and catching their breath.

"It's your mom," Mando whispered.

Hector looked over the hood of the car. It was his mom all right. She was holding a cutting from *Señora* Lopez's geranium. He looked at Mando and said, "Let's play a joke on my mom.

Watch this." He locked his lips and growled, "Meeooooooooow." ·

His mom and *Señora* Lopez looked around. When they didn't see a cat, they continued talking. After a minute, Hector again growled, "Meoooooow."

The women looked around, bewildered, and moved to the other end of the porch. They were now looking at a potted rose. Then Mando cleared his throat and barked, "Rooooar, bowwow."

The women didn't bother to look up. They were transfixed by the rose.

The boys laughed and gave each other a high five. Then Hector straightened up. "Hey, man, since we're here, I'm going to sneak home to get my swim trunks," Hector told Mando.

"Sneak home? Why don't you just go through the front door."

"Too easy, man," Hector said. "We can be like ninjas. Get in and get out without being seen."

Mando's eyes became dreamy, and Hector rubbed his hands together. Ever since Hector was a baby in diapers, he liked hiding from his parents — hiding behind doors, in closets, under piles of laundry, in trees and bushes. And once, he squeezed himself into a suitcase and had to cry for help.

The boys hurried away from the car and toward Hector's house. When Hector's dog, Smiley, woke and began barking, Hector scolded him and then hugged him.

"How you been, boy?" Hector asked as he patted him, rattling his dog tags. He let Smiley wash his face with his wet tongue.

They left Smiley and went around the back door and into the kitchen. They could hear the television in the living room and the snoring of Hector's father, tired from a day at work. They tiptoed through the kitchen, grabbing the last sugar doughnut from a cellophane-windowed box. Hector tore it in two and gave the smaller piece to Mando, who jammed it into his mouth and let the factory of teeth go to work.

"This is scary," Mando said in a low voice, licking his fingers.

"It's a piece of cake," Hector countered. "Come on."

They peeked into the living room. Hector's father was asleep, a snore rattling from his throat. The boys tiptoed past him, nearly laughing because the wind created by his snores was so strong that it moved the pages of the *TV Guide* in his lap. They tiptoed toward the bedroom, sweat once again dripping from their bodies. They closed the door behind them, laughing.

"Man, we're cool," Hector said.

"Smoooooooooth," Mando agreed.

Hector rifled through his drawer and pulled out a pair of huge orange-colored swim trunks, a bargain basement special his mother had found. He held them up to his waist.

"*Qué feo*," Mando said of the swim trunks.

"Yeah, but I figured you're in the water and nobody sees them, you know."

They started to leave when the boys heard the front screen door open with a sigh and his mother's voice, "*Viejo*, look what *Señora* Lopez gave me."

The snoring stopped. They could hear his father get up from the recliner. He mumbled something and his mother answered, "I'll put them in some water." His parents headed toward the kitchen.

"Man, we're caught," Mando whined. He looked at the bedroom window and said, "We can go out the window."

"*Chale*," Hector said. "Just follow me."

"Right from the frying pan into the fire."

They tiptoed into the hallway. Hector's heart beat loudly and his eyes were big with worry. He looked around the corner and could hear his mother scolding. "You ate the last doughnut?"

"No, *vieja*," his father argued.

"It was here when I left."

"I was sleeping."

"Eating in your sleep is the way it looks." They began to argue.

Hector eyed Mando and whispered, "We better get out of here."

They tiptoed out the front door and down the steps. Smiley the dog woke up and barked.

"*Cállate,*" Hector scolded. He patted Smiley and with Mando in the lead, they raced off down the street with the swimming trunks waving like a flag.

CHAPTER 13

The boys returned to the art opening, which had thinned to a few people nibbling on the few remaining carrot sticks. They offered a feeble explanation of why they had disappeared: they told Aunt Teresa that a dog had chased them for two miles — a half-truth. They left the gallery and returned home to listen to music, mostly Los Lobos and the nearly forgotten Malo. Just before bedtime, Aunt Teresa told the boys scary stories that weren't scary, except one about a woman who had coughing fits whenever she slept. The woman had a tapeworm inside her that wiggled around at night, and occasionally its head crawled out of her throat to peek around. The boys screamed as they remembered the wormlike noodles they had eaten.

The next day, after an uncomfortable sleep on a hard pull-out sofa, they woke up stiff, dressed, ate generous bowls of Cap'n Crunch cereal, and drove over to West Los Angeles. Aunt Teresa was still mum about what they were going to do, except that it involved the buckets of paint. Aunt Teresa pointed and said, "See that library?"

"Do we have to paint the library?"

"No, guys," Hector's aunt smiled as she turned the corner, the paint and ladders rattling in the back. "We're going to paint a mural."

"Us?" Hector asked. He thought that they were headed to the beach and was wearing his orange swim trunks under his jeans.

"Yes, you two Picassos," Auntie nodded.

"Auntie, me and Mando can't even color coloring books without going outside the lines."

"Don't worry," she answered. "You'll do just fine."

After Aunt Teresa parked the van, the boys hauled out the paint, spread a tarp on the sidewalk, and ate some *churros*, Mexican doughnuts, for energy. They whitewashed the side of the library building with fuzzy rollers on poles. Two other artists had shown up and rolled out plans sketched on butcher paper. The sketch featured a brown boy and girl reading books under a tree — a positive message about how enjoyable it is to read. In the background were rows of houses and cars round as potato bugs. In the sky was a plane with a banner reading *"Leer es poder./* Reading is power."

While the artists talked about the mural, Hector and Mando sneaked across the street to buy more *churros* and milk. Hector splurged, pulling out the wad of money he earned from the Band-Aid commercial.

"Those artists look skinny," Hector said.

"Looks like they haven't eaten in days," Mando agree.

They returned to the library and made everyone happy when they offered *churros* and milk. Aunt Teresa ruffled their hair and told them how sweet they were, which made their faces beam like flashlights.

Hector was told to paint the sky. He was handed a wide brush and a bucket of blue. Mando was told to paint the grass and given a bucket of green. The boys got to work, while Aunt Teresa and the artists penciled in the tree, the houses, the cars, and the plane. Everyone worked within earshot of a boom box playing oldies but goodies.

While Hector was up on the ladder, he looked west, sucked in some cool air, and smelled the ocean. He craned his neck and tried to see the Santa Monica beach, which he figured was no more than three miles away.

"Whatta you lookin' for?" Mando asked. His hands were totally green from the paint, and some of it even flecked his hair.

"The ocean."

"You can see it?" With his hand over his brow in salute, Mando looked in the direction Hector was looking. "I can't see nothing."

"I can't either, but I can smell the salt air."

The morning sun was less friendly now. It burned the backs of their necks, steamed up their hair, and stitched its way through their T-shirts.

"Maybe when we finish we can go to the beach," Mando hoped aloud.

"That'd be cool."

They worked quickly but carefully, and by noon they were done with their parts: the top of the wall was blue and the bottom was green. They stood back to admire their work and had to admit that kindergarten had taught them well.

"Hey," Mando said, "maybe your auntie will let us go now."

Hector gave a thumbs-up sign to Mando. He turned to Aunt Teresa, who was tracing on the almost-dried blue sky. She was penciling in the banner whipping from the tail of the airplane.

"Auntie," he called.

"¿Mande?" she responded, not looking up. She had one pencil in her hand and was biting down on another.

"Can we go down to Santa Monica? To the beach?"

"To the beach?" she said after she took the

pencil from her mouth. She wiped her brow and then, eyeing the boys and their hard work, said, "Sure. But let me finish this lettering."

While his aunt continued lettering, Hector and Mando crossed the street and bought burritos and sodas, another gift for the artists. They liked them. With their shoulder-length hair, their *huaraches*, their T-shirts that proudly blazed "Chicano Power!" they seemed cool. One was named Samuel, a student at Santa Monica College, and the other was named Oscar, a junior at UCLA. They were like brothers, like Hector and Mando.

"Where did you get all your money?" Auntie asked as she pulled her hair back and sat down on a milk crate.

"I was in a commercial," Hector answered before his jaws clamped down on a chorizo burrito.

"A commercial? *¿Cuándo?* When?" She took a burrito from Hector and peeled back some of the aluminum foil. A curl of steam rose up when she bit into it.

Hector told her the story of the girl who refused to fall and pretend to cry and how he stepped in to save the day. He had told the director that he was good at falling and that he would do it for next to nothing. Next to nothing was a hundred dollars and only two scabs on his knobby knees. Aunt Teresa laughed at his story and told the boys to hop into the van. The boys did as they were told and immediately hit the tops of their heads getting into the van. They yelped and laughed at their clumsiness.

As Aunt Teresa pulled away, her van popping from a bad muffler, she said, "What will you do at the beach? You don't have any swim trunks."

"I do," Hector said. He peeled down the lip of his pants and showed her his orange bathing suit.

"I'll just swim in my pants," Mando said. "I've done it before."

"You boys think of everything," she remarked and pulled onto Santa Monica Boulevard. She drove the three miles to the beach, repeatedly warning them that she didn't want them to wake up drowned.

"We'll be careful," Hector assured his aunt. "Mando and me know how to swim like penguins."

They drove in silence past burger stands and doughnut havens, past record shops, video arcades, and the umbrella-shaded ice cream carts. No temptation would alter their dream. They wanted to feel sand through their toes and the salty waves licking their backs. They cheered when they saw a fringe of the Pacific Ocean. They had been traveling for eight days with the hope of finally arriving at the ocean. Now they could not only smell the salt air, but see the waves too, white-tipped and roaring toward the beach.

Aunt Teresa pulled the van to the side of the road and warned the boys that if they drowned she would be really mad at them.

"Don't forget," she warned. "Watch out for the *tiburones*, those sharks."

Hector blew his aunt a kiss and said, "Don't worry. We'll be cool." When he jumped out of the van, he hit his head again on the door frame, another lump to remember his vacation by.

"I'll be back in three hours," she told the boys and pulled away, her battered van rumbling and popping as it cut in front of a Mercedes-Benz.

The boys waved, turned, and raced to the beach, which was crowded but not so crowded that they had to step over people. They were happy. They had journeyed for over a week and now they were churning over the heavy sand. Out of breath, they slowed to a walk and then slowed to a complete stop when they heard in the sea breeze, "Hey, you *vatos*."

Hector looked around. He asked Mando, "Did you hear something?"

"Yeah," he said. They looked around but didn't see anyone. There was just a seagull squawking at them.

"Hey, you dumb boys."

Now they knew the words were directed at

them. They looked at the seagull, which was rubbing its beak under the fold of its wing.

"Man," Hector whined, "someone is playing with us, Mando."

"I'm going to push their faces in the sand." Mando looked around, stern-faced and his hands rolled into hammers of anger. He hiked up his hands and stuck out his chest.

"Especially, you, Mando," the voice came again. "You skinny-legged dude."

"Who said that?" Mando screamed over the crashing waves.

Hector jerked his chin at Mando, indicating that the voice was coming from behind a striped umbrella. They tiptoed toward the umbrella and when they peeked around it, it was a shock that brought them to their knees.

"Hey, *vatos*," Sarah taunted. "I've been waiting for you since ten this morning.

"Sarah, what are you doing here?" Hector asked, his face sliced up into a pumpkin smile.

"Waiting," she said. She capped her bottle of nail polish and held up her feet, wiggling her toes in the breeze. "You told me you were going to be here."

Hector remembered crowing that he and Mando were planning to go to Santa Monica. He didn't dream that she would follow them.

"You dudes hungry?" she asked. She pointed

to a large wicker picnic basket with cheeses, crackers, fruit, gourmet peanuts, and club sandwiches lanced with toothpicks.

The boys looked at the food, big-eyed and with the buds of their tongues showing from their mouths. If they hadn't eaten the burritos earlier, they would have thrown their faces into this rich-person's grub.

"Nah," Hector growled. "We ate earlier."

"Good," Sarah said, closing the lid of the basket. "Because we're going surfing. You're not going to leave until I beat you and you're belly up on the beach!" She stood up with a leap, kicking a spray of sand into Hector's face.

This is Sarah all right, Hector thought as he rose to his feet, turned, and bumped into his Uncle Isaac, who was wearing orange swimming trunks identical to his own. A small nest of hair lay matted on Uncle's chest and goosebumps marched around his pale belly. He was cold and shivering without getting wet.

"Hello, Hector. Mando," he said with a nod, slighty embarrassed. "Chauffeuring has taken me to the beach, it appears."

"You look cool, Unc," Hector said. "We look like twins."

Mando hovered over the surfboards laid out on the sand. He turned to Hector and remarked, "Homes, this is gonna be hard."

"*Chale*," Sarah said. "You guys are top dogs. You can do anything."

Hector and Mando picked up their surfboards, not wanting to argue with Sarah, and dragged them toward the water. Uncle Isaac crossed himself in the name of the surf gods and, tugging up his swim trunks, followed the boys and Sarah. They walked across the hot sand toward the roped-off surfing area. They stood at the edge of the crashing waves that came to meet them.

"It's too cold!" Hector screamed.

"Come on, dude," Sarah shouted and flopped her board into the foamy water.

Hector shrugged his shoulders, walked into the ocean, and flopped his board on the surface of the water. He looked back to the shore, where the lifeguard was eating a candy bar and looking at a magazine. The lifeguard didn't seem to care, and the wave that slapped Hector when his back was turned didn't seem to care either.

"Here goes," Hector said. He jumped onto his board and began to paddle out to where the waves mounted, tipped, and curled into white water. A line of surfers all in wet suits, hair matted to their scalps, waited there. Hector thought they seemed to know what they were doing. One was standing up on his board, gliding along the push of a wave.

"Come on," Hector yelled to Mando and his uncle, who were still hovering around the shore, splashing each other.

"Come on," Sarah yelled in return to Hector.

Hector paddled out to the deeper water, his body chilled and his feet kicking through the sea kelp. Hector and Sarah hugged their boards, waiting for a big wave. The sun looked like a gold coin behind a haze of fog and cloud.

"So how you guys been?" Sarah asked, her eyes facing the sea.

"Pretty good. We've been painting a mural in West Hollywood," he began to explain. "It's a mural of — "

"Here's one," Sarah interrupted. She started paddling, and Hector followed suit, his arms crawling as his hands scooped water. Soon the force of the wave was upon them.

When Hector saw Sarah stand up, he did the same. His body wobbled left, then right, but his arms balanced him as he rode to the shore, yelling that he was free and that he could fly. And that's what he did: he flew right off his board into the white water where he turned over and over. He came up spitting a mouthful of salt water, a disgusting taste that stayed on his tongue.

"That's pretty good," Sarah congratulated.

"Yeah, I guess so," he agreed. "Let's try it again."

Hector and Sarah were joined by Mando and Uncle Isaac, both shivering like dogs. They waded far out where seagulls circled above and a chilly wind raked the water. They waited for another wave. When it came rising like a hand, they paddled, jumped into standing positions, and rode awkwardly. Uncle Isaac was knocked off the board first, then Mando, and then Hector. Sarah glided effortlessly toward the beach, queen of the surfers.

Mando came up spitting water and Uncle Isaac surfaced with a crown of seaweed on his head. They both smiled and said, "*Órale*, let's do it again."

Lying on their boards, chin up and maneuvering over the rise and fall of waves, they paddled out again into the deep water. They waited in silence as they straddled the boards. When a monster wave arose, Sarah shouted, "Last one to the beach is a *sapo*."

"*Simón*," Hector yelled over the roar of the wave. He paddled fiercely and got to his feet, but in the confusion of trying to keep upright, he saw that he was riding backwards.

"The other way, dude," Mando yelled.

"*¡Chihuahua!*" Hector screamed. But he stayed calm. He dug his toes over the edge of the board, prayed, and rode out the wave, the backwards champion of all time.

All afternoon they surfed and by the end of the day they were red-eyed from the salt water and ready to challenge the bigger boys and men. For Hector, this was the end of their vacation, one last spill in the source of all life — the ocean. He wanted to make the most of it, to live through every muscle in his thirteen-year-old body. He rode the waves over and over until Aunt Teresa arrived, kicking through the heavy beach sand and yelling that it was time to go home.

CHAPTER 14

The boys spent two days with Aunt Teresa, completing the library mural. Then, at daybreak, they biked back home, a long journey through smog, poor and rich areas, and centipedes of idling cars at each traffic light. They splurged on the way home and ate at a fancy seafood restaurant with starched napkins. When their salads arrived, Hector and Mando knew which fork to pick up, the smaller of the two. They knew how to use the finger bowl of lemon-scented water to clean up after a messy lobster meal. They had learned table manners from the two-day stay at Bentley's house.

And on the ride back, Mando bought a gold chain for his parents from a guy on the street. Hector had his Tommy Lasorda picture framed, a gift for his father, and at a rock-bottom price he snagged a ceramic poodle for his mother.

They were glad to get back to East L.A. and the bunk beds that the boys would share for a week because Mando's parents were now shaking hands with the slot machines in Las Vegas. They had seen plenty of Los Angeles and were now rich with memories — memories that brought them out of the house one morning, just as the dew on the grass was beginning to disappear.

"Let's go, homes," Hector commanded sleepy-headed Mando, who was wearing his T-shirt inside out. The word "Raiders" looked like Russian writing.

"What's the hurry?" Mando asked. He scratched his hair and peeled the rocks of sleep from the corners of his eyes.

"That," Hector said, pointing skyward to the sun peeping over the garage. During the past two days, there had been a heat wave that even slowed their otherwise busy and rascally cats.

Hector got an OK from his parents (mostly from his mother, who said it was better than graffiti) to paint a mural on the side of their garage. Hector had liked painting the mural on the library, and he figured that they should paint a mural to document the history of their bike ride. The day before they had sanded the surface, pried a few unsightly hunchbacked nails from the wood, and slapped on a base of white paint. Hector patted the surface, examined his palm, and muttered to Mando, "It's dry."

They hauled buckets of paint from the garage, and on the redwood picnic table they unrolled a long piece of paper and made a sketch: it showed Hector and Mando speeding on their bikes through the cities they had haunted — Maywood, Culver City, Beverly Hills, West Los Angeles, and Santa Monica. It showed family members and friends — Uncle Ricky wearing earphones, Bentley staring into a microscope, Uncle Eloy the engineer, and Aunt Helena the doctor cutting politely into *filet mignon*, Sarah with a bow and arrow and with her neck weighted down with Olympic medals, Uncle Isaac at the wheel of a limousine, and Aunt Teresa in front of the library with the *Leer es poder* banner overhead.

"It looks cool," Mando said, rubbing his chest in thought.

"Then let's go, bro'," Hector said, stabbing a paintbrush into the bucket and starting with the background of sky. "We got only two days."

They painted the sky while puffing up their cheeks and whistling while they worked. They painted a snake of freeway, a cluster of houses, Hector's dog Smiley and the three bad cats, and the "roach coach" on Brooklyn Street. They painted a scene of the Chinese cemetery and then mixed colors for the Mexican flag — the green, red, and white, with a little black for the snake.

After lunch, Hector's mom came out and helped with painting the beach at Santa Monica. She wore an old pair of rubber gloves and covered her hair with a red bandanna, which made Hector and Mando laugh. They told her she looked like a gang member.

"You should be glad I'm not," she scolded, clicking her tongue. "I'm your mommie." She busied herself painting a long tunnel of waves and singing to herself. She told the boys how she had always wanted to go to college to study art, and the boys said that it wasn't too late, that when they went to Loyola Marymount they saw a lot of old people.

"I'm gonna spank you bad boys," she laughed as she cut them a quick look through her bandanna, which had almost covered her eyes. "Calling your mommie an old woman. No respect!"

"Sorry, Mom," Hector said with a smile. "You're still tough lookin'."

They worked silently as they transformed the side of the garage into a fresco of neighborhood Chicano art. Hector's mom, finished with her duty, stood back, hands on her hips, unaware that the paint had dripped on her pants. Neither Hector nor Mando said anything.

"It's so pretty," Hector's mom said, pulling off her bandanna. "Everyone will be so happy." She placed the drippy brush on the lid of the paint can and went inside. She told them she had to start cooking for the dinner everyone was coming to.

"Everyone" was the family, and friends of the family, that she had invited to a *fiesta* on Saturday, a backyard *barbacoa*. After the return from their journey, Hector had told her one morning about how he regretted that his *familia* wasn't closer. When he shared his stories with his mom, she broke down while dunking a doughnut into her coffee. She told Hector that she missed her mother and father, dead for three years, and hoped that her half-brother Isaac would visit her. There had been squabbles over the years, in both his mom's family and his dad's family, and neither one of them was proud of it.

"And Ricky, Isaac, and Helena," she cried. "I miss them. I just see your *papi*'s family, but not mine."

To wipe away her tears, Hector told her how he snuck home to get his swim trunks and ate the last doughnut, which she blamed on Dad. Confessing, he figured that she would return to normal and get mad at him. Instead, she laughed and for punishment made him eat three doughnuts.

"Let's get *la familia* together," Hector had suggested, burping the sweetness of pastry. "We can have a party or something."

That was last week, when he rocked his mother as he tried to comfort her. Now they were dressing up the backyard with a mural. But instead of finishing it, Hector decided that each of the family members or friends would have to paint a picture of themselves.

"Yeah, that's a good idea," Mando said as he sat in the shade of the peach tree, a Kool-Aid stain at the corners of his mouth. "It'll be kinda like a game."

"You got any problems with your *familia*?" Hector asked as he lay on the grass, eyes closed, his hands folded behind his head. He was tired of painting.

"Shoot, where do I begin? My uncle Charly owes my mom three hundred plus a car."

"A car?"

"Yeah, we let him borrow our Nova, and we never saw it again. He said it got ripped off."

Fluttering his eyes open, Hector sat up, shook his head and said, "That's sorry."

They returned to work and the final touches, leaving a spot on each body where the faces would go.

The next day, Hector mowed the backyard lawn, pushed some new flowers into the ground, and scraped black grime off the barbecue grill. Mando helped him hose off the patio and set up the Ping-Pong table in front of the garage. When String Bean and *Masa* jumped onto the table and started clawing the net, Hector chased them away, threatening to make slippers out of them if they weren't careful. In the meantime, the third cat, Herman, bit holes in the Ping-Pong ball. Hector had to chase him away, too.

"Yeah, those are some bad cats," Mando said.

Then they returned inside to help Hector's mother scrub the bathroom, from the mildewed ceiling to the dark ring in the bathtub. Hector knew it was his ring but told Mando that it belonged to his father.

At three o'clock, the first guest arrived — Uncle Ricardo, the recording engineer, staggering into the backyard with a cardboard box of records and CDs.

"*Estoy aquí, hermana,*" he called. "I'm here, sis. And look what I brought for you."

The brother and sister hugged and rocked each other while Hector and Mando took a quick peek through the CDs. Uncle released his sister and bent down. He picked up some dusty records and twirled them on his thumb. They were all oldies but goodies — Sam Cooke, Aretha

Franklin, the Coasters, the Drifters, and the Chipmunks singing Christmas songs.

"*Mira*," he said, rifling through the box. "An album by that really oldie but goodie — Pedro Infante."

"Who's that?" Mando asked.

Uncle clicked his tongue and said, "*Pues*, you *escuincles* don't know *nada*! He was just the greatest Mexican singer of all time. Better than me even," he joked. He widened his eyes and said, "Hey, guess what, dudes, my main man is a rising star!"

The boys looked at him, confused.

"You know, dudes, Chilly Lagoon. We're selling his recording to Warner Brothers."

"No way," Hector said, waving his uncle off.

"*De veras*," Uncle Ricardo sang. "Go get a boom box, I'll show you how the song ended up."

Hector had turned to go into the house to get his blaster when he saw Bentley come up the walk with his mom and dad. He was dressed in a white shirt, khakis, and black tennis shoes. He was wearing one black glove on his right fist. He looked like a villager in this *barrio*, not the scientist they met in Culver City. Hector thought that maybe he and Mando had gone too far by turning him from a nerd to a little *vato loco*. But when he spoke, when he rattled his mouth, Hector could hear that he hadn't changed.

"Hello, Hector," Bentley chimed. "I got an A+ in chemistry."

"Hey, Little Benny," Hector greeted.

"You're lookin' baaaaad," Mando whistled.

It was the same Bentley, the brain-head with high math revolving in his head. They shook hands, *raza*-style, and then Hector greeted his *tía* Helena and *tío* Eloy by saying that he now knew the difference between the salad fork and the dinner fork.

"Hector, you're so funny," his *tía* Helena smiled, patting his cheek.

"Really, Auntie," he said. "Me and Mando learned a bunch of stuff on our trip. Huh, Mando?"

"Yeah, we got it down, Auntie. But I still got a problem with drinking glasses. Me and Hector went to a really fancy house and they had two glasses. Shoot, we didn't know which one to start with, so we used both!"

Hector and Mando laughed with their mouths open and punched each other in the arm playfully.

"Hello, Mando," *Tía* Helena greeted him after they quieted down.

Mando took her hand and shook it *raza*-style,

a twist of moves that left Auntie confused. Looking around, she asked, "Where's your mommie, *mi'jo?*"

Hector looked over his shoulder and turned. His mother was pouring lighter fluid on a pyramid of charcoal, while his father and uncle Ricardo were chipping ice with screwdrivers. Sodas were sitting in a large laundry bucket.

"*Ay,* my little sister," his aunt cried and hurried over with a *clip-clop* of high heels for a hug and kiss.

There were a lot of hugs and kisses, and some laughter that ripped like bedsheets through the late afternoon. Soon Aunt Teresa arrived, and Hector couldn't help but take her hand, begging her to look at their garage mural. He escorted her arm in arm to their two-day work of art.

"*Qué* pretty," Aunt Teresa smiled, then screamed with joy when Hector's mother touched her shoulder and turned her around for a deep *abrazo.* Then she hugged Uncle Ricardo, her baby brother, and Aunt Helena, her older sister. All of their eyes filled with tears, some from family sentiment and some from the smoke of the barbecue, which had flared up in jagged saws of fire.

"You like it?" Hector asked, leaning on Mando's shoulder.

"Yes, of course," she told Hector. She pulled at the corners of her eyes, wiping away the tears. She examined the mural. "But how come we don't have any faces?"

"Each of us is gonna paint in our own faces." Hector pointed and explained. "That's me and Mando on the bikes."

Just then Puppet pulled up on his bingo bicycle, which he had lowered by extending the frame. It was now metal-flake purple and sparkled with mirrors on the spokes.

"It's cool," Mando crowed.

"Yeah, *primo*," Puppet cooed as he hopped off the bike. "Can I have a soda? That was a heck of a ride from Echo Park to East Los."

Soon Uncle Isaac arrived, still wearing his chauffeur's cap. He brought along Sarah, who was hugging three bottles of sparkling apple cider in the crook of her elbow.

"Sarah!" Hector yelled as he hurried over.

"I'm glad that you invited me," she said, looking around. "Where can I put the dartboard?"

"Dartboard?"

"Yeah. I brought sparkling apple cider and darts. They go together."

"Like *frijoles y tortillas*," Mando joked as he tiptoed over with Bentley in tow.

"Yeah," she said, clicking her fingers. "Like

frijoles y tortillas, homeboys." She laughed, and her face brightened like a fistful of flowers.

Hector introduced Bentley, and Bentley introduced them to a sour lemon-flavored candy that he had made in chemistry. Their faces squeezed up into ugly masks.

"That's strong stuff," Mando remarked after the sourness disappeared from his coated tongue.

"I want to give them for Halloween," Bentley said.

The *fiesta* was on. The smoke from the barbecue clouded the air, and the laughter cleared the past of ill feelings. The dartboard was set up, and uncles and aunts began to paint their faces, all with big grins. And there was even a little spark of romance — Bentley eyed Sarah's muscles and Sarah complimented his brilliance when he added up the scores of the dart game without having to use his fingers. And neither Hector nor Mando got mad when Uncle Ricky slipped in the CD of Chilly Lagoon and explained that he couldn't use their refrain, *"nada más."*

Burgers and chicken were served with a splotch of *frijoles y arroz*. Hector's bad cats, those East L.A. *gatitos*, looked on as the knots of hunger began to untie. Forks began to rattle and laughter crackled through the air. In that back-yard, on that day, there was no room for family arguments. Peace had settled, along with the dusk, and the first distant stars began to wink over their good luck.

GLOSSARY

abrazo, abrazos — hug, hugs

ándale — come on

ándenle — come on, get over here

asco — sickening, nausea

un autógrafo — autograph

¡ay caramba! — (an exclamation)

Azteca — Aztec

barbacoa — barbecue

barrio — neighborhood

¿bueno? — customary telephone "hello"

¡cállate! — quiet!

carnal — friend, blood brother

chale — no way

chamacos — little kids

chavalo — child

chicharrones — fried pork rinds

chihuahua — (an exclamation)

chisme — gossip

chiva — goat

cholito — little cholo

cholo — low-rider

chones — underwear

chorizo con huevos — eggs scrambled with chorizo sausage

churros — doughnut-like pastry

claro, claro que sí — of course

cochino — pig, dirty

con — with

cuidado — be careful

cuando — when

¿cuándo? — when?

de veras — really, it's true

¿entienden? — understand?

¿entiendes? — understand?

East Los — East Los Angeles

escuincles — little kids

ese — guy

estos gatitos — these cats

estoy aquí — I'm here

familia — family

fiesta — party

frijoles y arroz — beans and rice

frijoles y tortillas — beans and tortillas

fuchi — smelly

gatitos — kittens

la gente — the people

gracias — thank you

helados — ice cream

hermana, hermano — sister, brother

híjole — wow

hola — hello

hombre — man

huaraches — woven sandals

jefe de los Dodgers — head of the Dodgers

lápices — pencils

¿loco o qué? — crazy or what?

¿mande? — What did you say?

mi — my

la migra — immigration officers

mi'jo — my son (affectionate)

¡míra! — Look!

el molcajete — grinding stone

molé con pollo — chicken in sauce

muchachos — boys, kids

mucho gusto — much pleasure, it's nice to meet you

muy bonita — very pretty

muy grande — very large

nada — nothing

nada más — nothing else

nalgas — buttocks

no sé — I don't know

novia, novio — sweetheart

La Opinión — name of a Spanish-language newspaper

órale — right on

palo — stick

pandilla — gang

pantalones — trousers

papas — potatoes

papi — daddy

patas — legs

perro, perrito — dog, doggy

placas — graffiti signatures

la playa — the beach

pobrecito — poor little guy

la policía — the police

porque como el maestro dice — because like the teacher says

prima, primo — cousin

pues — well

¿que? — what?

qué buena idea — what a good idea

¡qué feo! — how ugly!

¿qué más? — what else?

¿qué no? — isn't that right?

¿qué pasa? — what's happening?

¡qué pretty! — how pretty!

quesadilla — melted cheese in a tortilla

¿quién? — who?

¿quién es? — who is it?

¿quién sabe? — Who knows?

la raza — Latino people

¿recuerdas? — do you remember?

salud — bless you

sapo — loser, jerk

señora, señor — Mrs., Mr.

serape — shawl

sí — yes

siempre — always

simón — yes (emphatic)

su, sus — your

tía, tío — aunt, uncle

tiburones — sharks

turistas — tourists

un momento — just a minute

y todo — and everything

vámonos — let's go

vato, vatos — guy, guys

vatos locos — crazy dudes

véngan acá — come here

vieja, viejo — old woman, old man

About the Author

Gary Soto introduced the characters Hector and Mando in his book *Crazy Weekend*, which was well reviewed. His other critically acclaimed works include *Local News*; *Baseball in April and Other Stories*; *Living Up the Street*; and two collections of poetry, *A Fire in My Hands* and *Neighborhood Odes*. Mr. Soto has also produced three short films for Spanish-speaking children, *The Bike*; *Novio Boy*; and *Pool Party*, which won the Andrew Carnegie Medal for excellence in filmmaking.

Mr. Soto was born and raised in Fresno, California, and like Hector and Mando, he rides his bike daily.